Wake

Fairy tales and stories of wisdom, kindness, and compassion

2nd edition

Written by

NahMo

Illustration by

Ronald M. Cruz

ISBN: 979-8-987-39300-0

DEDICATION

To all beings,
May you be loved.
May you be at peace.
May you grow from your suffering.

Acclaim for Wake

"Simple, wise, heartfelt, and fun. These are lovely and insightful stories."

- *Jack Kornfield, Author, A Path With Heart*
  - ○ *San Rafael, CA, USA*

CONTENTS

ACKNOWLEDGMENTS

In early 2022, something profound happened. In fact, many critical events happened in my life in a short time. Although I was raised a Buddhist, hence taught to anticipate suffering, the waves of turmoil were hard to endure. In the wake, I sat with my suffering before I learned the purpose of its visit.

Suffering compelled me to pass on the lessons it left with me. To make some of the topics less gloomy for younger readers, fairy tales were chosen as the method for the narrative. The settings and characters of all the stories you find in this collection are imaginary composites of my childhood memories, stories my parents told me, dinner conversations with my husband, TV shows we enjoyed, and my isolated experiences at work. Each story stands on its own, but the main characters all converge on a singular message - we must find a way to be better in the wake of our suffering.

This book would not have been possible without the unwavering support and inspiration of my loving husband and daughter. They are my muses and the most encouraging test readers.

I am forever indebted to my parents for granting me a wonderful life and for teaching me how to be a decent human being.

THE PRINCE AND THE ANGRY DRAGON

Once upon a time, there was a kingdom in a faraway land. The kingdom was ruled by a king who was once a brave warrior. He conquered many battles in his early days. The king was a physically imposing man. It was said that an image of the king was used when lexicographers invented the word "masculine". His queen passed away many years before. She and the king had one son. The prince was not at all like his father. He was not fond of combat training or wrestling. He preferred to spend time in the library instead of on the sports field. The prince was small and skinny. His skin was pure and pale from the time spent inside the castle. Other young men his age were tanned and robust, and

3

the prince looked nothing like them. The king loved his son, but he was secretly embarrassed by how different his son was from him.

One day an angry dragon flew over the kingdom. It circled the town from above and breathed streams of fire into everything in its path. Villages were burned down. Forest fires were everywhere. The dragon was so furious that it did not care for the people's pleas for mercy. Everything was scorched to the ground.

The king sent troops to put out the fires and build shelters for the citizens. He sent a thousand of his best archers to shoot down the dragon. But the dragon's scales were so thick that no arrows could pierce through them. After all the arrows were spent, the dragon remained unscathed.

After a few days of fiery destruction, the angry dragon stopped to look for food and water. But since everything was pretty much destroyed, it decided to fly up to the mountain. But before it departed, it said,

"I will be back in three days. When I return, you must offer me a hundred men and a hundred women as sacrifices for my anger. Otherwise, you will see destruction like you never have before!"

The king saw this as an opportunity to regroup and plan a strategy to get rid of the dragon. He made a royal proclamation, offering a handsome reward to anyone who could come up with a way to eliminate the dragon for good.

After three days, despite long hours of consultation with royal advisors, military strategists, sages, and wizards, no one came up with a failsafe plan.

The prince observed everything that was going on. He tried to interject his opinions many times, but the king sent him away before he had a chance to speak.

"This is manly business," the king would say sternly before waving his son away in dismissal.

By the end of the third day, after all the consultants had left, the prince approached the king, who was still sitting on the throne. His head was buried in his hands. His body language spoke of despair.

"Father, I may have a way to get rid of the dragon. Please hear me out," the prince plead.

The king looked up and thought, "What's there to lose? Even a bad plan is still better than no plan at all." He then allowed the prince to speak.

The prince told the king his plan and asked for permission to carry it out. The prince asked for no troops and no special weapons. All he asked for was ten seamstresses to make ten gowns.

The king obliged and granted the prince ten seamstresses. The seamstresses worked all night and produced what the prince had specifically instructed them to. The prince then put on all the gowns, one over another. Because of his small frame, after the prince put on all the garments, he looked just like a regular-sized man.

When the morning came, the king and his troops were ready for the dragon's return. They were stationed far outside the city. The king sat majestically on his horse. Rows and rows of soldiers, archers, and calvaries lined up behind the king. Then everyone heard loud flapping noises in the air. When they looked up, they saw a dark figure fast approaching. It was the angry dragon!

The dragon made a deafening thud as it landed on the ground. The ground shook for several seconds before things settled down. The dragon slithered its way toward the king and his troops until it came face to face with the king.

"I see lots of soldiers but not one hundred men and one hundred women. Where are my sacrifices?" The dragon asked in an intimidating voice.

The king stood firm and responded.

"Dragon, we do not know why you are so angry. But my kingdom will not give up innocent lives for you. To make peace, would you instead consider —?"

Before the king could finish his statement, the dragon snarled, "No innocent lives? Well, well, well. You have brought this upon yourself. Now you and all your kingdom will get incinerated!"

The dragon then inhaled deeply to start the fire in its belly. It was about to breathe out the devastating fire when the prince boldly stepped in front of the king and said to the dragon.

"You are a coward! You are hiding behind layers and layers of protection and bullying people. I challenge you to a duel. But only after you take off all your body armor and reveal your true self."

The dragon pondered the challenge. This prince looked completely harmless. He was pale and delicate. It looked like he never exercised a day in his life! And he's wearing a gown no less! *This would be easy*, thought the dragon. Then it spoke.

"All right. I accept. But I will only peel off a layer if you do the same thing," the dragon said.

They shook on it and the challenge began. The dragon demanded the prince to go first, thinking this would give it an advantage.

The prince took off the first gown to reveal another gown under it.

"Your turn," the prince said.

The dragon shed its first layer of thick scales. Underneath there were lighter, more luminescent scales covering its body. The dragon looked a little smaller and less intimidating.

The prince took off the second gown. The dragon was upset that there was still another gown on the prince. But rules were rules, and the dragon removed one of its layers. Again, it looked smaller, and the scales were now much smaller and more like fish scales.

They took turns continuing the challenge. The prince took off a gown, then the dragon shed a layer. As the dragon took off the layers, it got tinier and appeared less and less like a dragon.

The prince still had two gowns on him when the dragon ran out of layers. It now looked like a small, harmless newt.

"So, this is who you really are, a newt," said the prince, "How did you turn into the angry dragon?"

The newt recognized that it had been exposed and it now regretted the challenge. It looked over a pile of layers it had shed off. It spoke as it slowly made its way toward the pile.

"When I was a tadpole, the lake I lived in dried up because the townspeople drained the water to use for their farms. I lost my home and my family. In grief, I built up layers and layers of rage and resentment. When I became a dragon and realized my powers, I sought revenge on the people who wronged me. But the grief did not go away, so I keep looking for more things to destroy."

The prince was saddened by the newt's story. He stooped down to the newt and said with great compassion.

"I am sorry about what happened. It must be very painful to lose everything that meant so much to you. I hope you can find it in your heart to forgive the townspeople, not for them, but for you. You deserve to be at peace, and you can end the destructive circle of anger and revenge right now."

The newt looked up at the prince, then looked at the pile of its former layers. The newt was so close to the pile now. If only it could put on all the layers again, it would turn back into the powerful dragon and it would once more gain the upper hand. It would not have to listen to anyone.

"I will never forgive!" The newt yelled out as it ran toward the pile of layers, trying to put one over another quickly.

The prince and the king and their men all stepped back on high alert. The king ordered his army to prepare for a fight of their lives.

But as the newt hastily put the layers back on, it did not get the order of the layers correctly. In a hurry, it put on the strongest outer layer before putting on the fire-resistant layer.

The newt now looked like the old dragon, but without a few important layers. The dragon started taking a deep breath to create a fire in the belly. It was ready to destroy everything with the flames of anger.

Alas, because the dragon did not have the fire-resistant layer on, the fire in its belly started to burn the dragon from the inside. The flames of anger quickly engulfed the dragon, who let out a terrible screech. After what felt like an eternity, the rage-filled fire burned the mighty dragon down to a mound of ashes.

The prince and the king looked at each other in amazement. In the end, it was the fire of anger and hatred that served as the dragon's undoing.

Before they turned around to head back to the kingdom, the prince walked toward the dragon's ashes. He muttered words of compassion to grant peace to the dragon in the afterlife.

When they all returned to the kingdom, there was a big celebration. Everyone was talking about how brave and clever the prince was, how he vanquished the dragon with wit, and how he compassionately offered the dragon a chance to repent. They talked about how the dragon was consumed by its own anger and how forgiveness could have saved its life.

The king was impressed by his son's actions and gained a new perspective of the prince. He embraced the prince's unique differences and showed interest in what the prince enjoyed doing.

Years later, after the king retired from the throne, the prince was crowned the new king. He ruled the kingdom with wisdom, kindness, and compassion. The citizens of the kingdom were happy and prosperous.

And they all lived peacefully ever after.

The End

Anger is often a package for another emotion. Sit with your anger in mindfulness until it tells you its true name. Address the core emotion and use the energy from anger as a motivation for positive changes.

Forgiveness is the cure for anger. While forgiveness is not easy to achieve, it will release you from the imprisonment of anger and guide you toward peace and light.

REAL MAGIC

Once upon a time, there lived a woman named Xiao Xiao. She was married at a young age. She lived with her husband and mother-in-law in a big house. When Xiao Xiao and her husband first fell in love, everything was beautiful. He tended to her every need and would not stop saying sweet words to her. Sadly, over the years, all the sweetness waned. And one day, the love he used to have for her turned into resentment and disgust. The man's mother, siding with her son, believed that Xiao Xiao was entirely to blame for her son's unhappy marriage. As a result, the mother-in-law was very cruel to her. Xiao Xiao had been taught by her parents to obey her husband and mother-in-law, so she never argued with them and continued to let them say and do mean things to her.

To survive the unkindness her husband and mother-in-law put her through, Xiao Xiao found refuge in the toolshed in the backyard. She took great pleasure in reading. She read everything she could get her hands on, and she kept many books in the toolshed. In particular, Xiao Xiao liked reading books about history and folklore. Sometimes, she would daydream that she was a character in one of the stories instead of being an unloved wife and unwanted daughter-in-law.

One day, her mother-in-law called Xiao Xiao to her room. When Xiao Xiao arrived, she knew there would be trouble. The mother-in-law was unhappy about something. The moment she saw Xiao Xiao's face, she approached her in a rush. She was holding a blouse in her hand.

"How do you call this?" The mother-in-law asked in a loud voice, shoving the blouse in front of her.

"I, I don't know what you are talking about?" Xiao Xiao honestly replied.

"Ai-yah! You are useless and stupid! This is my new blouse. You did not get the stain out completely. Incompetent dumb girl!" The mother-in-law furiously berated Xiao Xiao.

Xiao Xiao apologized to her mother-in-law repeatedly. She bowed and bowed and asked for forgiveness. The mother-in-law, who knew no kindness, continued to scold her.

After the mother-in-law was satisfied, she sent Xiao Xiao away. On the way back to the toolshed, Xiao Xiao saw her husband in the garden with a young woman. Her husband looked at the young woman adoringly, the way he used to look at Xiao Xiao when they first got married. She looked on with a broken heart. Her husband saw her but pretended she did not exist.

Xiao Xiao went back to the toolshed and cried. She felt helpless and stuck. Her life was completely miserable. She was wiping off her tears when she saw something strange. Sparks were forming on the floor inside the toolshed. The ring of sparks became larger. Bright white light shone from the center of the ring, then a figure emerged.

The figure floated towards Xiao Xiao, who stood frozen while witnessing the strange developments. As the figure moved closer, she could better make it out. It was a middle-aged woman in flowing, colorful, elegant robes. Her hair was put up in a complicated system of buns and hairpins. Then the woman gave Xiao Xiao a kind smile.

"Hello, Xiao Xiao. I am your fairy godmother," she introduced herself.

"Oh, he- hel- hello," stammered Xiao Xiao, still trying to understand what was going on.

"I have been watching all the cruel things your husband and mother-in-law put you through. That is not right. It needs to stop!" The fairy godmother said firmly.

A rush of hope came over Xiao Xiao. "Thank you, fairy godmother. Can you please use magic to get me out of here? I need to escape and go far, far away from them," she begged.

The fairy godmother paused for a moment and said, "No, Xiao Xiao. My magic is not going to help you."

"But you said this is not right and it needs to stop," Xiao Xiao protested, feeling confused.

The fairy godmother let out a chuckle. "You are correct. It is not right, and it needs to stop. And *you* will stop it. My magic won't work. It must come from *you*."

Xiao Xiao became visibly disappointed and said, "So, you came all the way here just to tell me that I have to get out of this horrible situation all by myself? I already know that!"

The fairy godmother retorted, "Of course, you do know that, but you've done nothing about it. *If you want to change your life, you have to be the one doing it.*"

The fairy godmother walked back toward the ring of sparks. Before she walked through, she turned around and handed Xiao Xiao a book.

"Take this book. I know how much you like to read."

She then disappeared into the bright light. The sparks started dying down before they went out completely.

Xiao Xiao was left holding a book. She tried to make sense of the visit from the fairy godmother. What kind of magic-less fairy godmother was that? Was that all a mean prank? Why did she even come here? If it wasn't for the book she was holding, she would have thought the whole thing had been a cruel dream.

That night, she read one chapter of the book. It was about civil laws. The book spoke about how to settle disagreements between neighbors and how to file lawsuits with the court. She fell asleep with the book on her chest.

The following morning, while doing her usual chores, Xiao Xiao heard her mother-in-law yelling from inside the house. Then she heard her name being called. She went inside, and once again, her mother-in-law was unhappy about something.

"Silly girl!" The mother-in-law howled the moment she saw Xiao Xiao, "Come over here at once!"

Then she showed Xiao Xiao a chipped bowl. The antique bowl looked expensive. Xiao Xiao knew something terrible was about to happen to her.

The mother-in-law continued, "You broke this! This, this is our family heirloom. How dare you disrespect our family? Did you do this to get back at me?"

Normally, Xiao Xiao would have just stayed silent, admitted guilt, begged for forgiveness that would never come, then willingly accepted the punishment. But then she remembered what the fairy godmother had said.

"If you want to change your life, you have to be the one doing it."

Xiao Xiao thought about what she had read in the law book last night and said, "I did not break your bowl. That chip looks like it happened a long time ago. You should not accuse me if you have no proof. I've read in a book of laws that you can be fined 100 gold taels for a false accusation. Do you really want to go there?"

Xiao Xiao could not believe what she had just said. But the person who was in more disbelief was the mother-in-law, who was trembling with anger. She was at a loss for words. All she could do was point her finger in Xiao Xiao's face. Her hand was shaking.

Xiao Xiao turned around and went back to her toolshed. It was a small victory. That night, she had a good sleep for the first time in a long time.

When the morning came, Xiao Xiao got up and opened the door, but it was locked. She rattled the door many times, but the door would not open. Someone had locked it from the outside. Then she heard a familiar voice. It was her mother-in-law's.

"Let's see what you are going to do about this now, Miss law book reader! Tomorrow my son and I will be out of town for a week. You will be in there and starve!"

Xiao Xiao heard her mother-in-law's footsteps retreat. She got down on her knees and cried. This was what she got for standing up for herself. She felt like she was a victim again.

Then the words of the fairy godmother echoed in her head.

"If you want to change your life, you have to be the one doing it."

She reached for the fairy godmother's book. She looked through the book and found a chapter about lock picking. She gathered the necessary tools and started unlocking the door.

It took Xiao Xiao many tries and finally, she got the door opened. As she stepped outside the toolshed, far ahead, she saw a man on a horse-drawn wagon waiting by the side of the road. Over the wagon, there was a sign that read "To the Capital". She decided to approach him.

"Good day, sir. I live over there," Xiao Xiao said, pointing over at the big house, "it's rather unusual to see a wagon on this road. I thought you might need directions."

The man replied, "You are very kind, young mistress. I am here to pick up the candidates for the emperor's advisor. His majesty has been looking for an advisor. He sent out thousands of wagons to transport promising scholars to the capital where they all will have an exam. The smartest scholar will become the emperor's new advisor."

Xiao Xiao had an idea. She asked the man the details about the exam and when the man would be back to pick up more candidates. He told her that his last pickup in this area would be tomorrow morning.

That night after everyone had gone to bed, Xiao Xiao got out of her bed quietly and tiptoed to her husband's wardrobe. She took out a few items and went out to the toolshed.

She used her sewing kit to alter the clothes to fit her body. The extra fabric was used to pad parts of the clothes to make her shape look like a man's. Xiao Xiao cut off her hair and tied it up in a small bun. She packed her personal items and the godmother's book in a bag. Then she waited inside the toolshed until the sun rose. Once the morning came, she got out and walked toward the road.

The man and the wagon arrived, and Xiao Xiao got on. Under her disguise, the man did not recognize her. He thought she was one of the ambitious young men who wanted to become the emperor's advisor. She read the fairy godmother's book from cover to cover and learned about many things on the way.

When Xiao Xiao arrived in the capital, she was inundated by the luxury and splendor around her. She had never seen such sophistication. It would be a dream come true if she could live here.

After registering for the exam, one of the officials showed her to a modest room where she would spend the night. Xiao Xiao studied all night to get ready for the exam in the morning. When she woke up, Xiao Xiao was led to an enormous hall with hundreds of identical desks. All the scholars were assigned to sit at each desk. When everyone took their seats, the exam began.

Xiao Xiao finished the exam before everyone. After she handed it over to the officials, she walked out of the hall, wondering what to do next. Then she saw a young boy wandering the ground by himself. She walked over to him and asked, "What is the matter? Why are you by yourself?"

The boy looked up and told her that he sneaked out of his class because he didn't want to study. The history teacher was mean to him and what he taught was boring.

Xiao Xiao laughed and said to the boy, "History? Boring? That can't be. I love history. It is the best!" Then she began telling the boy about the history of the past dynasties. She made the stories engaging, lively, and relatable to the boy. The boy listened to her attentively and lost himself in the stories. When she finished, he clapped his hands in delight.

"That was so much fun! I want you to be my teacher. Please be my teacher!" The boy cried.

Then suddenly, he looked up and exclaimed, "Father! Meet my new teacher!"

Xiao Xiao turned around to see the emperor standing behind her. She cast herself down on the ground and greeted him.

"Your majesty," said Xiao Xiao, her head bowed low.

The emperor smiled and said, "I have been listening. And I, too, enjoyed the stories you told my son. He will find learning fun with you as his teacher. How do you feel about becoming an imperial tutor?"

Xiao Xiao was over the moon. She graciously accepted the position. She told the emperor and the prince the truth about her identity, how her husband and mother-in-law were cruel to her and how she finally escaped. The emperor offered to severely punish her husband and mother-in-law, but Xiao Xiao asked the emperor to spare them.

From then on, Xiao Xiao lived a happy and peaceful life in the palace. She thought of her husband and mother-in-law often, but not about all the merciless things they did to her. She thought of how their cruelty transformed her into a brave survivor, how she found herself through all the suffering, and how it shaped her to be who she eventually became.

And that's the real magic.

The End

In life, suffering happens. As painful as it is, sometimes suffering is necessary magic. It transforms us into who we are meant to become. Buddha, Jesus, and Moses all suffered greatly before they became the magnificent men that they were. Through mindfulness, we can grow from our suffering. We will find that the most satisfying accomplishment comes from what we have suffered through, and not from what comes easily to us.

THE SQUIRREL AND THE DOG

Not long ago, there lived a squirrel who was carefree and happy. His home was in a big pine tree in a deep forest. He made friends with small birds and other tree rodents. Life was simple and peaceful.

That was until one day when a man and his wife built a log cabin in the forest by the pine tree. The man and his wife owned a hunting dog. Every day the man would leave the cabin with his dog and his crossbow. His wife would keep the house and tend to their tomato garden.

A few weeks passed and the garden was filled with all kinds of tomatoes. The squirrel looked at the tomatoes with amazement.

"How convenient! An all-you-can-eat food source right outside my doorstep," he thought to himself.

Every day after that, the squirrel would sneak down from the pine tree, pick a few tomatoes, and take them back to his home. At first, the man and his wife did not notice the missing tomatoes. But as time went on, the squirrel became bolder and took many more tomatoes. After a while, there were only few tomatoes left in the garden.

The man and his wife concluded there must be a thief in the area. The man put his dog outside at night by the garden to watch over it. The dog was attentive to the task and stood watch diligently. The squirrel made note of this development and stopped frequenting the garden for tomatoes.

The squirrel went back to his usual diet of pine nuts. But it did not take long before he started thinking about the juicy tomatoes from the garden. Compared to the succulent tomatoes, the pine nuts tasted bland and dry. The more the squirrel thought about the tomatoes, the more he wanted them. But what to do about the dog?

Then he had an idea.

One night, a bright full moon decorated the sky. The squirrel approached the dog as the dog stood guard by the garden.

"Ahem. Excuse me. Do you work here?" the squirrel asked.

The dog glanced at the squirrel and growled, "Who's asking?"

"I am a neighborhood squirrel. I live up in the tree over there. I saw the tomatoes in the garden and thought I might buy them from you," the squirrel replied.

The dog gave the squirrel little attention and said, "These tomatoes belong to my master and mistress, and they are not for sale. How are you going to pay for them anyway?"

"What a shame!" the squirrel cried, "I was going to pay for the tomatoes with a map for buried treasures. But since you speak so authoritatively on your master's behalf, I'll just move on to the next tomato farm with my offer."

The dog gave it a quick thought. *"Treasures for master and mistress? They'd think I'm such a good boy for closing this wonderful deal!"*

The dog then said to the squirrel, "Where is the treasure you are speaking of?"

"No. No. No payment until I get to pick as many tomatoes as I want," said the squirrel.

The dog was not sure what to do. What if the squirrel was lying? He'd be giving the tomatoes away for nothing. But what if the squirrel told the truth? He'd miss out on this incredible opportunity.

The squirrel noticed the dog's reluctance and said, "All right. I can show you a glimpse of the treasure. If you look east, beyond the grove of oak trees, you'll see a sparkling spot in the clearing."

The dog looked over in the direction. Beyond the grove, something was glittering just like the squirrel said.

"I guess you are right. Feel free to help yourself to the tomatoes. Now that I can see the treasure, I don't think a map would be necessary," the dog said happily, then he darted off.

Not long after the dog was out of sight, the squirrel quickly ran into the garden and picked up as many tomatoes as he could. He put some in his mouth, under his armpits, and tucked a few under his chin. Then he climbed back up to the tree to put the tomatoes away and came back down for more.

The dog started running in the direction of the shimmering light. He ran past the grove of oak trees. He saw a clearing ahead. He could see the shimmering getting closer and brighter.

When the dog reached the clearing, he saw a big lake with a reflection of the bright moon above. All the glitter he'd seen earlier was just a big moon! The dog knew he'd been fooled by the squirrel. He ran back to the garden as fast as he could.

While the dog was gone, the squirrel made many trips to the garden and helped himself to all the tomatoes. By the time the dog returned to the garden, all the tomatoes were gone.

The following morning, the man and his wife woke up to a bare tomato garden. Next to the garden was the dog with his head lowered, avoiding direct eye contact with his masters.

"How on earth?" the man uttered, looking around with astonishment.

As it turned out, after weeks of eating stolen tomatoes, the squirrel had a habit of leaving tomato seeds in patches on the ground. All the tomato seeds now grew into small tomato plants. The man would have many more tomatoes in the coming weeks. He was pleased with this discovery.

The man put up fences with protective nets around the garden and new patches of tomatoes. He put the dog back on hunting duties.

The squirrel no longer had free access to the tomatoes. He pondered another scheme but could not come up with anything.

One night, the squirrel was examining the fence around the tomato garden to see if there was a way to break in. That's when he heard a growl behind him.

"Remember me?" the dog snarled, showing his glistening sharp teeth.

"Oh dear," the squirrel cried, trying to run away but the dog had him by the tail.

"I am sorry I lied! I just wanted the tomatoes so much. I didn't know what came over me. Please let me go," the squirrel begged.

The dog chuckled and said, "It was wrong for you to trick me, but it turned out Master now has more tomatoes than ever. Thanks to you."

"So, we are good? Let me go?" the squirrel asked, feeling some relief.

"Not quite," replied the dog, "I have a proposition for you. Now that they have more tomatoes than they can eat, some go rotten, and they throw them away. And I do not like wasting food."

The squirrel turned up its nose and said, "I know where this is going but I don't eat rotten tomatoes. Thanks, but no thanks."

"Who says anything about giving you rotten tomatoes?" The dog got a little irritated. Then he continued, "I can give you fresh tomatoes every week if you agree to one thing."

"And what is that?" the squirrel asked, getting worried.

"Here are some seeds. I want you to plant them for my masters. You turned out to be quite a gardener," the dog said.

The squirrel gave it a thought and said, "Ok. I can do that. But how many tomatoes do I get in return?"

"We'll start with one tomato a week. If you do a good job, we can negotiate your raise," said the dog.

The squirrel wanted to make a counteroffer, but then he realized that the dog still had him by the tail. It's either one tomato a week or sudden death. The choice was obvious.

"Deal!" the squirrel agreed.

From then on, the dog gave the squirrel all kinds of seeds to plant. The squirrel proved to be a talented gardener. He perfectly spaced out the seeds and transplanted seedlings when they were too crowded. He planted lettuce atop carrots to keep the weeds down. He paid attention to irrigation and fertilizing the soil. Everything grew beautifully.

Week after week, the man and his wife were delighted to see new crops emerge. They enjoyed various kinds of fruits and vegetables, unaware of how they came to be.

The squirrel and the dog continued their business relationship. The squirrel did such a good job that the dog soon gave him unlimited tomatoes every week.

And they all lived peacefully ever after.

The End

Things aren't always what they appear. What we first think of a person may turn out to be wrong. What initially appears to be a misfortune may turn into an opportunity for growth. With the right mindset, adversities can turn into successes, and enemies can become allies.

THE TWIN HOUSES

Once upon a time, there was a king who was known for his passion for beauty. The king surrounded himself with beautiful things, beautiful animals, and beautiful people. His castle was known for its grandeur and luxury. People from far and wide traveled to the kingdom to experience its splendor.

When visitors arrived at the kingdom, they were greeted by delicately sculptured statues at the entrance. Colorful majestic flags flew high above the gates. Inside the gates and throughout the city, there were flowers that bloomed at different times of day and night. The trees were lush and manicured, and the landscapes were precise. All the homes and buildings were constructed with architectural sophistication and adorned with complementary colors. Nothing looked out of place. Exquisite artifacts were found on every street corner. The entire kingdom was like a giant museum. It was the biggest attraction of its time.

The king took much pride in his kingdom and its glory. Every week, he would go out with his entourage to inspect the city and its perfection. The king had sharp and critical eyes. He would uproot plants at the earliest sign of illness. He would tear down structures if they seemed esthetically out of place and promptly build new ones on top of the ruins. Houses and buildings would be immediately repainted if the colors were off by even the slightest of shade. Displeasing objects were covered up by more visually delightful replacements. This practice kept the kingdom beautiful, but its people were constantly under a great amount of stress. The citizens were always on edge because, as everyone knows, maintaining picture-perfect beauty is serious business.

One day, on his weekly surveillance, the king and his men traveled far toward the border of the kingdom and noticed two identical houses. They were separated by a narrow path and looked like mirror images of one another. The houses were dilapidated on the outside and heavily wrapped in thick vegetation. The king could not stand to look at the atrocities for a second longer and ordered the men to tear the houses down.

The king's men set to work. To their astonishment, the houses were built with rock-solid materials. The foundations were deep and strong. The pickaxes and hammers wouldn't even give the houses a scratch. By the end of the day, the two houses stood untouched. This gave the king much distress. He wanted the houses gone, demolished, razed to the ground! How could he bear to live with these blemishes in his perfectly beautiful kingdom? He felt a tension headache coming on.

After the king returned to the castle and took some aspirin, he thought of an idea, *"If I can't tear down the ugly houses, I shall make them beautiful!"*

The following morning, he issued a royal search for the best house remodeling team in all the land. There were many applicants from within the kingdom and faraway countries. The applicants were given preliminary tests to certify their skills and taste levels. After many rounds of competitions, there were down to two teams – team alpha and team omega.

The king could not decide which team should be the sole winner. Since there were two ugly houses, he assigned a house to each team. They each had one week to complete the makeover.

Team alpha started the project by ordering beautiful paint pigments made of rare minerals, ivory, and shells of colorful creatures. They sent men on fast horses to Afghanistan, India, and China to make sure they had the right shades of pigments. Once the paints were made, the painters set to work. Each color was laid on with accuracy. With each step, the designer of the team would ensure that the colors were complimentary and most visually pleasing.

Team omega also took to the task quickly. But to the king's surprise, team omega did not ask for special materials or paints. They worked with what they had brought to the competition. Team omega spent all their time, day and night, removing vegetation and dirt, cleaning and scrubbing the inside and outside of the house.

Every day the king sent his men to monitor the work progress. The men would report that team alpha was busy with the colorful paints and décor and their house looked more and more stunning each day. All team omega was doing was scrubbing the walls and the floors of the house.

"Maybe this is just the cleaning crew. The interior decoration team may be arriving." The king wishfully predicted team omega's strategy.

Toward the end of the week, there were still no signs of the additional crew for team omega. The king became worried and thought he should just end the competition now and ask team alpha to finish the job on both houses. But he gave his royal words, and his better judgment told him to wait until the week was over. Nonetheless, the suspense kept him up every night.

The week of anticipation and sleepless nights had gone by, and it was now time for the big reveal. After consuming a large pot of coffee, the king arrived at the site of the competition. All the people in the kingdom were there to see how beautiful the houses would look and who would be declared the ultimate winner.

Each house was covered by a large canvas that was held up by enormous scaffolds. After the crowd settled down, the king ordered team alpha to reveal their finished project.

Team alpha pulled down the canvas to reveal a vibrant and colorful structure. The outside was painted with rich earth tones and harmonizing trims. The stencils of mythical animals on the outside walls were lifelike and alluring. When the king entered the house, he was greeted by a symphony of vivid colors. It was like a dream. Each room had a different theme. The murals on the walls told classic stories of courage, love, and heroism. The king immersed himself in the house for a long time. The king's advisor had to remind him there was another house to look at.

The king reluctantly walked out of team alpha's house. He thought there would be no way team omega could surpass the wonder he had just witnessed.

Everyone gathered around outside team omega's house, the king was in front of all of them. Then he ordered the canvas to be pulled down.

Team omega removed the canvas. Underneath was a glorious house made of marbles and precious stones. All the exterior walls were accented by inlaid gold. The surface of the marbles captured all the spectrum of natural light and radiated shimmers of various colors. Everyone gasped in amazement. The king took several minutes to collect himself, then he entered the house.

The inside of the house was even more magnificent. Besides the shimmering marbles that made up the walls, the ceiling was made of tens of thousands of crystals, forming patterns of the milky way and all the constellations. The floor was made of shiny onyx that reflected everything above it. When the king walked inside the house, it felt like he was walking on water or floating in the night air. Each room was adorned with different jewels - one room was emerald green, one was topaz yellow, and one was ruby red. When the king entered the last room, whose large windows opened to directly look out on team alpha's house, he was mesmerized by the purity of the white marbles that formed the walls. The marbles were so pure that the king could see the reflection of team alpha's house on them.

The king was very impressed by what team omega had accomplished. He sent for the team's foreman. When the foreman appeared in front of him. He asked, "Tell me, how did you pull this fabulous job off without asking for more materials? Where did all the marbles, gold, crystals, and jewels come from? All these must have cost you more than the prize money for the competition would."

The foreman humbly said, "Your majesty, we did not order any of the precious materials because the house was originally built with them. The house was covered up by layers of vegetation and years of dirt and mud – hiding its true beauty. My crew only revealed what's already there."

The king was surprised and pleased by the answer. He proclaimed team omega the clear winner of the competition and rewarded all the team members handsomely. The king commissioned them to remove all the paints in team alpha's house and restore it to its original glory. When all the work was done, the twin houses quickly became the biggest attraction.

This experience changed the king's view on beauty. The king continued with his weekly tours of the city. But now, when he saw something unusual, instead of tearing it down or covering it up, he would pause and consider its natural beauty and true value. He stopped the practice of removing and replacing and focused on restoring. Things were allowed to grow and fade naturally because there's beauty in just being. The people became happier and less tense. And as the layers of stress and tension peeled away, the citizens showed their natural kindness and love for one another. And that's the most beautiful thing of all.

The End

> *We are born with the purest and most precious nature. Although time and life struggles may add layers of impurities to conceal it, at the core, our lovingkindness and compassion stay intact and bright. Uncover the layers of negativity and allow your true nature to shine unapologetically through. The world deserves to witness the beauty that is you.*

*This story is inspired by Rumi's "The Chinese and Greek painters".

HOW TO STOP A BULLY

Chai hated going to school. He used to love learning, but after he entered the fourth grade, everything changed.

A new student joined the class, his name was Joe. Joe transferred from another school. He was much bigger and older than the rest of his classmates. It was rumored that Joe had repeated the fourth grade at least twice, and he was moved from school to school because of bad behaviors.

Chai soon found out the rumor was, in fact, true. Joe was mean and unruly. He disrupted the teacher constantly and spent more time at the headmistress's office than in class. During recess and lunch, Joe was nowhere to be found. No one knew where he went.

Sometimes he returned to class. Sometimes he did not come back at all.

After a few weeks, Joe started harassing other students. He would tease them and take their things and never return. Chai tried to avoid Joe as much as possible, but somehow Joe paid most attention to him. Perhaps that was because Chai was different. Chai was small for his age. And when he was born, one of his feet was not fully formed. The doctor made him a pair of special shoes. Despite the shoes, he still walked with a little limp. Chai had never thought that this was a flaw until Joe brought it up repeatedly when he mocked him.

"Nice shoes, weirdo!" Joe would say as boisterously as possible so everyone could hear.

Most other students would look on and pretend they did not hear anything. But some boys, trying to be on Joe's good side, laughed along when Chai was harshly teased.

Since no one seemed to have enough courage to stop Joe, he got bolder. And as he got bolder, more boys joined his gang. Chai tried his best to be invisible at school, but Joe and his entourage seemed to always find him. The more Chai tried to hide, the worse the taunting became.

Chai told his parents once about the bullying. His parents went to the headmistress, who called Joe's parents in for a conference. After the talk, things were quiet for a few days. Then, not only that the bullying reappeared, but it also became more severe and frequent.

Chai dared not tell anyone about how much worse things were.

Chai pretended to be sick to stay home. He forged a fake field trip permission slip so he could stay out of school. Because Chai had always been a good student, his parents and his teachers never suspected his deceit. But after so many days of school absence, his grades got noticeably worse. His parents were worried about him and tried asking him what the problem was. Chai still remembered what happened the last time he told on the bully, so he kept quiet.

Due to his failing grades, Chai's parents became stricter with him. They made sure he would not miss a day of school. This put Chai in much anguish. He hated going to school. He hated being called mean names. He hated being different. He hated being himself.

A few weeks later, the headmistress announced that a new teacher had joined the school. Mr. G was young and handsome. He had a fun and goofy teaching style. It did not take long before he became the most popular teacher in the entire elementary school. Mr. G got to know almost every student, and he noticed that Chai was withdrawn and sad. He also noticed how intimidating and disturbing Joe and his gang were to other students.

One day, Mr. G asked to speak to Chai after school.

"Hello, Chai. How is school going for you?" Mr. G asked.

"It's ok, I guess," Chai answered, avoiding direct eye contact with the teacher.

Mr. G said, "Is there anything that bothers you? I looked at your records. You were a wonderful student last year. But since you started the fourth grade, your grades have been, well, concerning."

"I am ok. Maybe I am just not smart. Can I go now?" Chai asked.

Mr. G sighed. He told the boy that he was always available if Chai wanted to talk, then he let him go.

As Chai was leaving the school, he saw Joe and his gang waiting for him. His heart sank. *"Here comes the torture,"* he thought and braced himself for the worst.

But just before Joe and his friends could launch their verbal insults, Mr. G showed up behind them. Joe and his entourage stopped in their tracks and ran away.

Mr. G walked over to Chai and compassionately said, "Look, I know those kids bully you. I am sorry that they make your life difficult at school. I can report them and talk to their parents. But that only puts a stop to it for a while. You can do something about it too."

Chai looked up at Mr. G with a mixture of sadness and frustration and asked, "What can I do? Look at me. I am small. I walk funny. I can't even run away from them fast enough."

Mr. G sat down next to Chai. He smiled and said, "That is actually where we will start. We will start by changing how you see yourself."

They talked for a long time. Mr. G offered to walk Chai home. They continued talking until they both reached the boy's home. Mr. G chatted with Chai's parents for a bit, but he said nothing about the conversation he had with Chai.

The chat with Mr. G gave Chai an idea. Over the weekend, he went to the store and bought a few things for the following school day.

Monday arrived and Chai went to school. Nothing seemed out of the ordinary. When the bell rang at the end of the day, Chai stopped by Mr. G's desk and told him his plans.

Chai walked out of class. He saw Joe and walked confidently toward him. This caught the bully by surprise. He was not used to being approached by one of his victims. As Chai walked closer, Joe noticed that Chai was carrying a bag and one of his hands was inside it.

"Hello, Joe," Chai said confidently as he looked straight at him.

"What do you want?" Joe asked, getting a little worried. This was all so unfamiliar. *Why was Chai not running away from him? Why did he not look scared? Did he know something Joe did not?*

What's Chai holding in the bag?

Then Chai said to him,

"I've been thinking about you bullying me. I know I am different, but that shouldn't bother you. I don't think you bully me because you hate me. You do it because you hate yourself."

At this point, more students and teachers were gathering around them. Mr. G was among them.

Chai kept addressing the bully,

"Your words convinced me that my difference was my weakness, and you made me hate myself. But guess what? I don't give you that power anymore. I love me and everything about myself. Your words will never, ever change that." Chai said, clutching an object inside his bag.

"Whatever!" Joe said loudly, pretending to look exasperated. He began to notice the crowd forming around them. Some of his gang members were in the crowd.

Chai moved his hand inside the bag, then went on, "I have something for you. This is what you deserve."

Joe became alarmed. *Was it a pepper spray? A taser? A knife?* He wanted to run away but did not want the gathering crowd to see what a coward he was.

Chai reached into his bag. Joe feared the worst. He covered his face with both hands and yelled out, "No! Please don't hurt me!"

Chai pulled his hand out of the bag slowly. He was holding a card. He said to the bully, "Here, I got this for you."

Joe reluctantly took the card.

"Read the card!" One of the students yelled out. Then more joined and they all yelled, "Read the card!"

"Read the card! Read the card! Read the card!" the students and the teachers joined the chant.

Joe slowly opened the card and read,

"Weak people put others down, strong people lift them up. Don't be a bully. Be someone's hero."

Mr. G yelled out, "That is right, Joe. You can do it. You can be a hero!"

The students and the teachers applauded. Joe looked confused.

Chai walked away from the crowd. Mr. G was waiting for him.

"Good job!" Mr. G congratulated Chai.

Chai thanked Mr. G for listening to him and for being his inspiration to act against the bully. Other students slowly joined them. They congratulated Chai for his bravery.

"Chai, you are a hero!" One of them said.

From then on, Joe stopped bullying other students. Without the leader, his gang eventually dissolved. Chai loved going to school again. He formed an anti-bullying group at school called "Be a Hero", with Mr. G as the advisor.

The End

Our natural response to fear is to avoid it. This instinct keeps us safe. However, avoidance is not a sustainable practice when what we fear continues to persist. The longer our fear lingers, the more power it has over us. In the end, we must use courage to face the fear head-on and conquer it to reclaim ourselves.

Note to readers

If you are bullied or know someone who is being bullied, please speak up and seek help. Bullying is never acceptable. Understand that you are not the problem and that the bully may indeed need help too. Talk to your parents, teachers, principals, or other school officials. You can go to stopbullying.gov for more information.

We can all be heroes!

THE RUNNING BOY

Once upon a time in a land far away, there lived an orphan boy. His parents died when he was a baby, and the boy was raised by his grandmother. The boy and his grandmother owned a small farm with chickens, ducks, goats, and a cow. The boy helped his grandmother with the farm work diligently. His grandmother loved him very much. She would make sure that he had nutritious meals and good education. She would not allow the boy to skip school, not even for half a day.

One day, the grandmother became ill. The boy wanted to stay home to take care of her. But the grandmother begged the boy to go to school. Being the obedient child that he was, he agreed. To take care of his grandmother and attend school at the same time, the boy would prepare breakfast for his grandmother, take care of the livestock, then run to school. Every recess and lunch break, he would run back home from school to check on his grandmother and the animals. When he was sure they were all okay, he would run back to school before the school bell rang.

The school was quite far from the house, but this did not dampen the boy's determination. The boy would run back and forth many times throughout the day, and this went on for many, many days.

One day, as the boy was running back home on his morning recess, he came upon a flapping sound. As he looked closer, he saw a duck flapping its wings frantically. It appeared the duck had been caught in a trap. The trap held one of the duck's legs to the ground and it could not fly away.

The boy slowly approached the duck and said in a calm and gentle voice, "Don't worry. I won't hurt you. I will set you free."

He reached down and carefully released the duck's leg from the trap. The duck let out a "Quack!", flapped its wings, and flew away. The boy went back home, prepared lunch for his grandmother, then ran back to class.

The following day, as the boy ran home on his lunch break, he heard a cat crying in distress. He looked up a tree and saw an orange cat on one of the tallest branches.

He climbed up and when he got to where the cat was, he reached out his hand and the cat immediately walked into it. It clung to his back as the boy climbed down the trec. When they both got down to the ground, the cat jumped off the boy's back, let out a "Meow!", then ran away.

The following day, as the boy ran home from his afternoon recess, he came upon an old man. The old man was sitting by the side of the road. He looked tired and weak. The boy stopped and asked the man if he needed help.

The old man said, "Dear boy. I haven't had any food or water for days. I came to town for a new job, and I was unfortunate enough to run into a few robbers. They took everything from me and left me in the woods. I walked for many days until I found this road."

The boy felt deep compassion for the old man when he heard the story. He then said to the man kindly,

"Elder, if you don't mind a measly meal, you can have my lunch." He handed over his lunchbox and water container.

The old man was very touched by the boy's generosity. He reached out and took the food and water.

"Thank you very, very much. You are very kind." The old man said with genuine gratitude.

The old man started eating and drinking hungrily, then he asked, "why are you running around like this in the middle of the day?"

The boy then told the old man how his grandmother got sick and how she didn't want him to miss school. It was then that the boy realized that he would have to get back to class soon. Before the old man could say anything, the boy quickly said goodbye and ran off toward the house. He checked on his grandmother and the livestock, then ran back to school.

The following morning, the boy was preparing his grandmother's breakfast when she called out to him in a soft voice,

"I don't feel well today, grandson. I think I need a doctor."

The boy wasn't sure what to do. There were no doctors for miles and miles around. The nearest neighbor lived a few miles away. He decided to go there to ask for help.

The neighbor took the boy on his horse and dropped him off at the capital. The boy begged the neighbor to look after his grandmother until he returned. Then he talked to every doctor in town. All the doctors said they did not know how to cure the boy's grandmother. When he arrived at the last doctor's clinic in town, the doctor said,

"I am sorry I cannot help, but I heard the new royal doctor is very knowledgeable. He will be able to help. But this will cost you a lot of money.

The boy's heart sank. The royal doctor lived inside the palace. How would he get inside? And even if he could see the royal doctor, how would he pay the doctor's fee?

Amid his despair, he thought of his grandmother and how she depended on him. He was her only hope. There was no time for despair. The boy gathered up all his courage and went to the palace guards. He pleaded desperately to them to see the royal doctor.

"No one gets through these doors," the guards said sternly.

The boy was disappointed and sad. As he turned around to leave, he saw a sign posted by the doors. The sign read "Reward for anyone who can bring back the king's lost dreams and the queen's joy."

Then the boy heard, "Quack! Quack!"

He looked around and saw the duck he saved the other day. In the duck's beaks, there was a little cricket.

He walked closer. Then the duck spoke.

"Thank you for helping me the other day. This cricket lives outside the king's bedroom window. The king listens to the cricket to fall asleep and has good dreams. The cricket escaped, and the king stopped having dreams. Bring the cricket to the king and he will have his dreams back."

The boy was moved by the duck's gratitude. He took the cricket and thanked the duck. The boy then went to the guards.

"I am bringing back the king's dreams. Please let me in," the boy said.

The guards let him in and showed him to the king's adviser. The boy handed him the cricket and told the adviser what the duck had told him.

"Is that so?" The adviser asked, skeptical, "I will have to check with his majesty about this. Wait here." The adviser said as he brought the cricket inside to present to the king.

As the boy was waiting, he heard, "Meow!"

He turned around to see the orange cat he'd rescued from the tree the other day. In the cat's paw, there was a mouse. The mouse was holding a diamond earring.

He walked over to the cat and the cat said,

"I am forever grateful for your help. This thief stole the queen's earring. It is a very important earring because it's the first gift she ever received from the king. She lost all her joys when she lost it. When the adviser comes back out, tell him you are also here to bring back the queen's joy. He will certainly let you meet the king and the queen."

The boy took the earring and thanked the cat who ran off after he released the mouse.

While the boy was talking to the cat, the advisor presented the cricket to the king and told the king what the boy had told him. The king was amazed.

"Of course, the cricket sound. That's what has been missing. I'll be sleeping well tonight!" the king cried with delight, then he thought of his queen's missing joy.

"Find out if the boy knows how to restore my queen's joy. If he can, we will give him anything he wants," the king declared.

When the advisor returned, the boy showed the advisor the earring and told him what the cat had instructed him to.

"The queen's earring for her joy?" the advisor asked curiously.

The boy told the advisor about how he saved the cat and how the cat caught the mouse to repay him.

"What an extraordinary young man!" the advisor exclaimed, "I will show you to his and her majesties at once."

The boy followed the advisor to the royal hall. The king and the queen were elegantly seated on their respective thrones. The queen was pleased when the advisor presented her with the lost earring. The king and queen asked the boy what he would like as a reward.

"I only want the royal doctor to cure my grandmother, please, your majesties," the boy humbly asked.

The king summoned the royal doctor. When the doctor entered the royal hall and saw the boy, his eyes widened.

"Dear boy!" the doctor cried with excitement.

It turned out the royal doctor was the old man the boy gave lunch and water to the other day. The royal doctor ran toward the boy and gave him a tight hug. The king and the queen traded each other puzzled looks.

The doctor explained to the king and the queen what had happened - how the boy ran to school and back home many times a day to care for his ailing grandmother, and how generous the boy was to give him food and water when he himself had very little.

The king and the queen were very impressed by the boy's actions and integrity. They permitted the doctor to leave the palace to take care of the boy's grandmother. They provided the fastest carriage to take the doctor and the boy to his home, as well as a caravan of supply carts filled with medicines and foods to accompany them.

The boy and the doctor got home in no time. The doctor tended to the boy's grandmother and every day she felt better and better.

When the grandmother's health was fully restored, the royal doctor invited her and the boy to move in with him in the palace. The doctor taught the boy everything he knew about medicine. Because the boy never missed a day of school, he was able to learn everything quickly.

Years later, the boy grew up and became a doctor. He took over the royal duties and served the king and the queen for many, many years.

And they all lived in peace ever after.

The End

There are so many things we can learn from the extraordinary running boy - kindness, dutifulness, perseverance, and integrity, to name a few. Integrity means always doing the right thing, even if it is difficult, or even if it may lead to repercussions.

How do we know what the right thing is? When you seat yourself in a place of kindness and wisdom, you will always find what the right thing is.

THE THREE PRINCESSES

Once upon a time, there was a king. The king had three daughters. The oldest daughter was renowned for her beauty. Kings and princes from near and far sought her hand in marriage, but the princess remained undecided. The middle daughter was known for her magnificent singing voice. It was said that when the princess sang a sad song, the whole kingdom wept. The king was very proud of his first two daughters.

Now, the youngest princess was not famous for anything. She was often dressed in plain clothes. She did not like putting on makeup. She never claimed to have special abilities. Her father was not very fond of her and thought she was simple. This did not bother the young princess at all.

One day, the king received words that the prince of the most powerful kingdom would be visiting his castle. He was certain that during the visit, the prince would fall in love with one of his daughters, well, just the first two. Who would look at the youngest princess in her plainness and think, *"I'll marry her."*?

When the prince arrived, the king instructed his daughters to stay in their chambers. The king welcomed the prince with gigantic feasts. The foods represented all the cuisines one could possibly imagine. The prince was entertained by the music of many different genres and perfectly synchronized dancers. At night, a thousand fireworks went up in the sky and turned the night sky so bright it looked like a day in summer.

When the festivities started to subside, the king spoke,

"My dearest prince. We are honored that you chose to visit our kingdom. I'd like to present to you my daughters the princesses."

The three princesses appeared. First to enter was the oldest princess, followed by the middle princess. The youngest princess made her entrance last. Everyone was stunned by the oldest princess's beauty. Then the middle princess started singing. No one bothered to question why she suddenly broke out in songs because her voice was so stunning. It put the audience in a trance.

The youngest princess kept to herself in the back of the hall. *"It's my sisters' time to shine,"* she thought to herself and felt proud of her sisters for their special abilities.

The prince was delighted by what he saw and heard. But his attention was focused on the youngest princess who stood far behind the crowd. Even though her sisters had the spotlight, the youngest princess looked truly joyful for her sisters. She smiled brightly when the crowd marveled at her oldest sister's beauty. She clapped and laughed when her other sister sang and enchanted the crowd. Not a trace of envy or bitterness could be seen.

The following day, the prince said to the king, "I would love to ask one of your daughters to be my future queen. They are all extraordinary. I will need to ask them a question to make the decision."

The king was very pleased to hear that the prince wanted to marry one of his daughters. "By all means, dear prince, you can ask them whatever you wish," said the king.

The prince asked to speak with each of the three princesses in private. He asked to meet with the oldest princess first. When she arrived, he showed her a diamond-encrusted hand mirror, a music box made of solid gold, and a bag of grains. Then he asked the princess to choose one of the three objects. The oldest princess picked up the hand mirror. The prince asked her why.

"So I can see how I look and keep up my beauty for you, my lord," the oldest princess answered, hoping the response would please the prince.

The prince thanked her and asked if she would let the middle princess in.

When the middle princess entered the room, the prince showed her the same three objects and asked her to choose. The princess chose the music box. The prince asked her why.

"So the music can add to my voice when I entertain you, my lord," she answered, crossing her fingers behind her back.

The prince thanked the middle princess and asked her to send her youngest sister in.

The youngest princess walked into the room. The prince immediately noticed her natural beauty behind plain clothes. The prince showed her the three objects and asked her the same thing he'd asked her sisters.

The youngest princess looked at the three objects carefully. Before she gave him an answer, she said, "May I ask you a question?"

The prince gleefully said, "Of course, I was hoping someone would!"

The youngest princess then said, "The hand mirror and the music box are both luxurious and expensive. What is the bag of grains doing here? It seems out of place. Is there something special about it?"

The prince smiled, "This is no ordinary bag of grains. The grains are magical. One grain can grow food that feeds a village for an entire year."

The princess was pleased with the information. She picked up the bag of grains and said to the prince, "This is my choice."

The prince asked her why. The princess smiled at him and said, "Why do you ask a question that you already know the answer to?"

The prince knew right then and there that he'd found his future queen, but he said nothing. He thanked the youngest princess and bid her good night.

When dawn broke, the king requested an audience with the prince.

"Have you made a decision?" the king asked the prince. He was trembling with excitement.

"Yes, your majesty, I have," the prince replied. He then asked that the three princesses join them one at a time.

The oldest princess arrived first. She was self-assured of her beauty and thought that her choice of the hand mirror was very practical and appropriate.

The middle princess followed. She believed her choice of the music box was clever and very applicable. As she joined her oldest sister, they both looked at the king, who looked back with confidence.

Then the youngest princess entered. Instead of her normal plain clothes, she was dressed in an elegant gown. Her light makeup perfectly complimented her facial features. She was stunning.

The king and the two older princesses watched with astonishment. The prince, on the other hand, looked unsurprised. He gave the youngest princess the most charming smile and held out his hand.

"Your majesty, I would like to ask for your blessing to marry your youngest daughter," the prince said.

"Wait. Wha-, wha-, what did you say?" the king stammered. He pinched himself repeatedly to make sure he was not in some sort of a multiverse nightmare.

It took the king a few seconds to collect himself. Then he incoherently said, "Of course. Yes. Sure. That's. My daughter. My youngest daughter. Yes. You. Marry her."

The prince took the youngest princess's hand. He handed her the bag of magical grains and said, "You selflessly chose what's best for the people. That's the most important quality I was looking for in my future queen."

He looked at the youngest princess adoringly and she looked back at him with deep affection. With her makeover, she outshone the oldest princess in beauty.

The prince said, "I am the luckiest prince in the world. My future wife is not only kind, but she's also beautiful."

The youngest princess smiled playfully and said to him, "Well, I don't want to brag but I can sing and hit higher notes than my other sister by an octave. You indeed have chosen the best."

The prince took his future bride back to the most powerful kingdom. They had the biggest wedding in the history of man. The celebration went on for many, many weeks.

The magical grains were distributed equally between the two kingdoms. Both kingdoms enjoyed years of plentitude and prosperity.

Many years later, the prince and the princess became the king and the queen of the most powerful kingdom. And they lived blissfully ever after.

The End

Physical qualities are subjected to fade over time. Kindness, on the other hand, is lasting and continues to multiply the more we exercise it. We are all born with an incredible capacity for kindness. Discover the kindness within you and immortalize it by sharing it with the world.

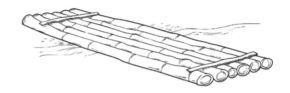

THE RACE DOWN THE RIVER

Once upon a time in a distant kingdom, there lived
a rich man. The rich man had a daughter whom he loved
very much. He named her Dharika – meaning baby girl.
He hoped to find a suitable husband for her - someone
of the same wealth and social stature. Dharika, however,
was in love with a man who owned a small shop in the
market. Because the man she loved did not have much
money and he was of a lower social class, Dharika did
not dare tell her father about her dreams to marry him.

One day, the rich man asked to speak with Dharika in
private. When she arrived at his study, the rich man said,

"You are old enough to get married and have your own
family. I have selected three suitors from wealthy
families for you to choose from. The three eligible men

will be here tomorrow. I want you to consider them carefully and choose one of them to be your future husband by the end of the day."

Dharika kept silent. She wanted to tell her father that she had given her heart to the shop owner in the market, but she could not. The tradition at that time dictated that parents had the right to arrange marriages for their children. In the end, she nodded slightly in agreement and excused herself to go back to her room.

Back in her room, Dharika felt miserable at the thought of marrying someone she did not love. Her handmaiden tried consoling her, but that did not help. Dharika cried so much that the handmaiden's heart was breaking for her. The handmaiden then made a suggestion,

"Young mistress, if you don't want to go through with your father's plan tomorrow, I will help you escape. And you can be with the man you love."

Dharika pondered the suggestion. At first, she thought of her duties as a daughter. Then she thought of her lifelong happiness with the shop owner.

Finally, she stood up and told the handmaiden, "Let's do it!"

Later that night, when the clouds covered up the bright moon and the twinkling stars, the handmaiden let Dharika through the back gate of the house. They walked along the deserted path so they would not be seen. They kept walking all night. By the morning, they arrived at the handmaiden's hometown. Dharika removed her expensive attires and put on plain clothes.

She took off all pieces of jewelry and gave them to the handmaiden as rewards. Dharika walked back to her town and found the shop owner in the market. Even in plain clothes, the shop owner recognized his love immediately and they embraced. Dharika told him how she had disobeyed her father and escaped. The shop owner was moved by the risks she took so they could be together. He asked her to marry him, and she agreed.

Later that day, they got married in secret. They moved to a different town. The shop owner built them a small cottage. After seven years, they had two children together.

One day, the shop owner noticed that Dharika looked sad. He asked her what was bothering her.

"I miss my father. It has been years since I last saw him," she said with melancholy.

The shop owner was not sure if it was a good idea to face the rich man after all they had done. But he loved his wife, and he could not bear to see her sad for another minute. He agreed to take her and their two children to visit Dharika's father.

The following morning, the shop owner put their luggage on a horse-drawn cart. After everything was loaded, all four of them got on the cart and took off. The road was rough, and the sun was blazing. They made a stop by the river to rest. The shop owner went down to the river to get water for his family.

After a long while, the shop owner did not return. Dharika got curious and took her two children down to the river to look for her husband. When she reached the riverbank, she found a trail of blood and his torn clothes. There were footprints of a large tiger nearby.

Dharika cried out and collapsed to the ground when she realized her husband had been killed by a tiger. Her children were too young to understand what was going on. Though her heart was broken, Dharika's head told her she and her children could not remain by the river, for the vicious predator might soon return. She wiped off her tears and quickly led her children back to the cart. They got back on the road and headed towards her father's house.

She did not stop crying until they arrived at the rich man's house the following day. To Dharika's surprise, her father's house looked deserted and empty. She asked the neighbors if the rich man had moved. One of the neighbors recognized Dharika and said to her gently,

"Poor child. I am so sorry to tell you this. But after you ran away years ago, your father became so sad that he could not eat or sleep. He stopped taking care of his health and his business. Last year, he got so sick and passed away. The house has been abandoned since then."

Dharika was devastated by the terrible news. She broke down and cried like no one had ever cried before. She felt the weight of all the world's sorrow. All the voices around her became mumbles and her vision got blurry. Then everything went dark, and the world became dead silent and numb.

From that day on, Dharika barely spoke to anyone. She rarely slept or ate. She continued taking good care of her children, but she had no vitality. Every night, she would pray to the gods to bring her husband and her father back, then she would cry herself to sleep.

Her prayers were heard by Yama, the god of Death. Yama was impressed by her devotion. He decided to pay her a visit under the guise of a yogi. One night, he went to Dharika's home and knocked on her door. When she answered, he spoke,

"Mistress, I cannot help but hear your prayers about your lost husband and father. I think I may be able to help."

Dharika kept silent, uncertain what the yogi's intentions were. Then the yogi continued,

"I can help you get your husband and father back to life. It won't be easy, but it can happen if you follow my strictest instructions."

"Another scammer," Dharika thought. She was about to dismiss the yogi when she noticed that even though she could see the yogi's face clearly by the bright light from inside the house, there was no shadow behind him. She recognized at once that the yogi was indeed the god of Death.

Dharika got down to the ground and groveled in deep respect. Yama knew he had been exposed and turned into his divine form.

"Poor woman," Yama said, "I am moved by your suffering. I will grant you one chance to bring your husband and father back to the land of the living. Meet me tomorrow by the river. And bring both of your children."

Dharika praised and thanked Yama profusely. When she looked up, he was gone.

The following morning, she took her children down to the river and waited for Yama on the pier. Soon she noticed a man on a raft floating down the river. Behind him was another raft. The man stopped when he saw Dharika. He got off the raft and tied both rafts to the pier.

"Greetings. Thank you for meeting me here," said the man who then transformed into the god of Death.

Yama said, "Here's the deal. I will take your husband and father on the first raft with me. You will get on the second raft and follow us. If you can catch up and bring them on your raft and return here, you can have them back in the land of the living. Your children, however, will remain on the pier."

Dharika agreed. Yama got on his raft and waved his hand. Suddenly Dharika saw her husband and father on his raft. They both looked at her and cried out her name.

The sight of her husband and father gave Dharika so much hope. Dharika said goodbye to her children and got on the second raft. Yama untied both rafts and all of them sailed down the river.

At first, the water was slow and peaceful. Dharika was able to match her pace with Yama. But after a while, the current got stronger. Dharika did everything she could to keep up. Every time she got close enough to reach for

her husband and father, Yama pulled away. The current became stronger and stronger, and Dharika's raft started chipping away.

She did not give up. She kept pushing forward to maintain a close distance. She almost reached her beloved so many times but did not quite make it. She tried and she tried. Her raft kept breaking up. Her husband and father looked back at her with worried looks. Her raft kept getting smaller and smaller, but Dharika kept going. With one big push, she got very close to Yama's raft. She reached out to her husband.

Her husband looked back at her lovingly, recognizing she would not be able to take him and her father back on her raft that was quickly disintegrating. He said to her,

"My love. You must let us go. If you kept on, you would drown and would never return to the shore to the children. Our children need you."

Dharika kept pushing the raft forward and cried, "Please. I cannot lose you again!"

Her husband smiled and said, "You will never lose me. No one can take what we have, not even Death. I will always be in your heart."

Then the god of Death pulled away down the river. Dharika's raft could not hold up any longer. The raft broke off in pieces and she fell into the raging water. When Dharika was able to get above the surface, Yama's raft was nowhere in sight. Her husband and father were once again gone for good.

The river raged and Dharika struggled in the water. She felt deep despair. She wanted the river to take her. She wanted the pain to end.

Then she thought of her children – the children she left by the pier. They were by themselves, and they needed her. She summoned every ounce of strength she had and started swimming. She swam with all she got against the powerful stream. She grabbed onto everything and anything that came her way just to stay above the water. The river swallowed her down, but she pushed her way back up to the surface. She kept swimming until she got to the shore. Then she ran as fast as she could toward the pier to look for her children.

The children were there waiting for her. Their faces lit up with joy when they saw her. When she got to them, she held them tight in her arms and let out a cry of mixed emotions.

She failed to bring her husband and father back, but she was able to reunite with her children.

How joyful. How heartbreaking.

How beautiful. How ugly.

How unfair. How real.

How a human life ought to be.

After a good cry, Dharika wiped off her tears and got up. She glanced back at the river one last time. Then she looked at her children and gave them the most loving smile that only a mother could. The children watched her face like she was the only thing that mattered in their world.

Then Dharika took the children's hands and all of them walked home.

The End

Dharika suffered great losses. She tried her best to hang on to what was lost. She was swept into the river of sorrow that only pulled her deeper into it until she learned to let go. And only by letting go, was she able to find her way back to the shore where life's new meanings were waiting for her.

CROSSING THE BRIDGE

Long ago, there was a town situated at the foothill of a large mountain. There was a big river that ran through the town, separating the town into the west side and the east side. There was one bridge that connected the two sides of town. Being the only throughway over the river, the bridge was very busy. And to make matters worse, the bridge was quite narrow. There were two small lanes, one heading east, the other heading west. Endless streams of people, animals, and vehicles lined up to cross the bridge every day.

On the east side of town, there was a merchant who owned a grocery store. His name was Karim. Karim made a good living selling grocers to people on both sides of the river. He would cross the bridge a few times a day to deliver the goods to the people on the west side.

Karim had lived in this town for a long time and had figured out the best time to cross the bridge. As a result, he managed to avoid traffic for the most part. He was known for quick deliveries, and his business prospered.

One day, another merchant came to town. He chose to set up a grocery store on the west side of town. The new merchant's arrival brought nothing but anger and frustration to Karim.

"Who needs another grocery store in this small town? This new guy is totally out of line. He is going to steal all my business on the other side of the river!" Karim thought to himself.

Karim was so flustered that he could not sleep at night. He decided to visit the new merchant to try to figure him out. He showed up at the new merchant's store pretending to be one of the customers. He picked up a jar of preserved fruits and said to the new merchant,

"I heard there's a much better and bigger store on the other side of the river. It's a shame you did not know about it before you decided to open this tiny little store."

The new merchant smiled and said to Karim,

"Sir, I indeed know of the other store. I think it's a good thing for the customers to have choices. The people on the west side will be able to get essential household things without having to cross the bridge. Besides, a little competition can't be a bad thing."

This rubbed Karim the wrong way. *"Competition?"* he thought, *"how dare this young man thinks he can compete with my store?"*

Karim then revealed who he was and said to the new merchant,

"Young man, competition implies that both parties are on an equal footing. Your puny store clearly is no competition with my big store."

The new merchant remained pleasant. He tried to properly introduce himself to Karim. But Karim did not want to prolong the conversation. He put the jar of preserved fruits back on the shelf and left without saying goodbye.

That night, Karim tossed and turned in bed. He kept thinking of a way to get rid of the new merchant. Then a thought came to him.

The following morning, he went over to the bridge and waited for the new merchant. The new merchant arrived and waited for his turn to cross the bridge. Karim made note of the time. Karim stayed by the bridge all day. He wrote down all the time of the day the new merchant crossed the bridge. After a week of observation, he had the new merchant's commute schedule precisely documented.

Over the same week of spying, Karim built an enormous wagon and loaded it with the heaviest goods he had in his store. He hitched two horses onto the wagon and rode it toward the bridge. He timed it so he arrived at the bridge right at the same time the new merchant waited to cross from the other side.

Karim moved his wagon forward and parked it right in the middle of the bridge. The wagon was wide and occupied both lanes. Not only did the wagon block the new merchant's way, but it also prevented everyone from getting through from either direction.

People started yelling at Karim to move his wagon out of the way. But Karim's attention was fixed on the new merchant on the other side. The new merchant noticed Karim but continued to look calm and collected. He did not seem at all bothered by Karim's antics. No matter how much the townspeople begged, pleaded, or threatened Karim, he wouldn't move the wagon.

The new merchant finally gave up and turned around to go back to his store on the west side. Karim laughed out loud in victory. When the new merchant was completely out of eyeshot, Karim slowly backed his huge wagon off the bridge. The traffic on each side resumed. But Karim did not leave the area. He parked his wagon nearby, waiting.

In the afternoon, the new merchant returned to the bridge with his cart filled with merchandise. Karim saw him and quickly urged his horses to pull the wagon over the bridge. Once again, Karim's wagon blocked the traffic right in the middle of the bridge. The new merchant looked a little exasperated this time. After a few moments of waiting, the new merchant retreated and headed back to the west side. Karim was pleased that he finally was able to annoy the new merchant.

For many days, whenever the new merchant wanted to cross the bridge, Karim would be right there to block his way. Each time the new merchant would turn around and return at a later time, only to find Karim's big wagon blocking the bridge again and again.

Karim blocked the bridge traffic many times a day. Because he spent all his time by the bridge, he neglected to buy fresh produce and restock his goods. When customers arrived at his store, they saw overripe fruits and rotten vegetables. Almost everything on the shelves was beyond its expiration dates.

A few weeks passed and Karim stopped seeing the new merchant at the bridge. He was ecstatic. *That young man finally gave up. I won!* Karim thought.

Karim, without a doubt, had succeeded in preventing the new merchant from crossing over the bridge to the east side. But the success came at high costs. Because of the poor quality of Karim's products, the customers stopped showing up at his store. His reputation also suffered. The townspeople realized he was an unreasonable and selfish man. They did not want to have anything to do with him.

Not long after, Karim went out of business and had to sell his grocery store to a businessman who turned it into a restaurant. Karim was out of work. The businessman was kind enough to hire him as a dishwasher at the new restaurant.

Despite being prevented from crossing the bridge, the new merchant's business was not at all hurt. His store flourished even more after Karim went out of business. Being the only grocery store to serve both sides of town, people on the east side traveled to the west side to shop at the new merchant's store. The new merchant no longer had to travel across the bridge. As his business expanded and he made more profit, the merchant donated a large sum of money to build another bridge for the town.

As for Karim, he learned a valuable lesson. He spent the rest of his life washing dishes and vowed never to wish ill on anyone ever again.

The End

> *The law of karma reminds us that we are all connected. When you treat people badly or get out of your way to hurt someone, the negativity always finds its way back to you. And when you feel joy when others succeed, the same joy is returned to you in multitude.*

THE SPARROW AND THE HAWK

A little she-sparrow lived in a forest with her mate.
The two lovers made their home in a hollow of a beech
tree. The forest was lush and peaceful. There was plenty
to feed, and predators were rare. Life was pleasant.

One early spring, the she-sparrow laid two eggs. The
she-sparrow and her mate were overjoyed to become
first-time parents. They took turns tending to the eggs,
day and night. When one had the nest duties, the other
would forage and bring back food.

One morning, the male sparrow left the nest to look
for food. The she-sparrow was keeping the eggs warm
when she noticed a green snake slithering its way up the
beech tree. Hoping the male sparrow was not yet too far

from home, the she-sparrow cried out for her mate as the snake approached the nest. When she realized that her mate was too far to hear her call, she defended her nest ferociously. She fluttered her wings forcefully, trying to scare the snake away. But the snake did not retreat. The snake tried to strike the little sparrow many times, but luckily for the sparrow, the snake missed. The she-sparrow did her best to protect her eggs, but with all the commotion, one of the eggs rolled off the nest and fell to the ground.

Without thinking, the sparrow instinctively dove down after her egg. Alas, by the time she neared the ground, she saw the fallen egg had already broken. It was just then that she thought of the other egg in the nest. The other egg was unguarded, and the vicious snake was still there! Panicked, the sparrow flew up to her nest as fast as she could. But when she got to the nest, both the snake and the remaining egg were nowhere to be seen.

The she-sparrow was distraught. Within seconds, she lost both of her eggs. She lay still in her nest, feeling empty and sad. How would she tell her mate about the terrible losses they had suffered today?

Dusk came, and the male sparrow still did not return. The she-sparrow waited and waited. Then she decided to leave the nest to look for him.

The she-sparrow flew from tree to tree. All the while she let out a "chirp-chirp-chirp" call to let her mate know she was looking for him. She asked every animal on her way if they had seen the male sparrow. None of them could help her. When she reached the edge of the forest, she met a squirrel. The squirrel told her about a hunter who was in the forest earlier today. And when the hunter left, it looked like he had caught a few birds. The squirrel did not know for sure, but he was quite confident that one of the trapped birds was the male sparrow.

The sparrow's entire body was heavy with sorrow. In less than one day, she lost her entire family. She did not remember exactly how she managed to return to her nest, but she did. She spent the night staring blankly into the night sky.

In her grief, the she-sparrow stayed still in her nest for many days. At first, other sparrows came by to drop off food. Some tried to strike up small talks to cheer her up, but none of them stayed long. No one knew what to say to the grieving sparrow to make her sadness go away. After a while, the image of her unrelenting despair made all the other sparrows uncomfortable, so they stayed away.

One day, a hawk flew by the beech tree where the sparrow's nest was. With its sharp vision, the hawk could see a small sparrow sitting deep in her nest inside the tree hollow. The sparrow was not moving much at all. The hawk got curious and decided to fly over to investigate.

The sparrow saw the hawk landing on a branch right outside her nest. She was alarmed. *"Does he think I am lunch?"* she thought to herself. The sparrow was very weak from days of not having enough food. She would be easy prey for the hawk.

The hawk moved closer to the sparrow's nest and then peeked inside the hollow. There was no way for the little sparrow to escape. She closed her eyes and prepared for the worst.

"Hello there!" the hawk said. He sounded oddly cheerful.

The she-sparrow opened one of her eyes. The hawk was right in front of her face. If he had wanted to eat her, it would have been easy and quick for him.

"What, what do you want?" the sparrow asked reluctantly.

The hawk responded, "I was just flying by, and I saw you in your nest. I thought you might be sick or need help."

"A helpful hawk? Now I've seen everything." the sparrow thought. She was still skeptical of the hawk's true intentions. She thought it would be best to convince the hawk to go away. With her eyes keenly fixed on the hawk, she said, "I am doing just fine. Thank you for your concerns. You should be on your way now, though. I don't want to keep you."

"Alright then. Take care," the hawk said, then he flew away.

The sparrow was relieved. *"That hawk must have just eaten something. That's why he didn't want to eat skinny little me."* she thought to herself. Then she figured she should start finding food and getting stronger, in case the hawk returned with an empty stomach.

She flew out of the nest to look for food for the first time in a very long time. She found grains and small worms. After she was full. She looked for twigs and feathers and brought them back home to repair and fortify her nest. She put a few pieces of bark to cover the tree hollow so the nest wouldn't be so easily visible.

The next day, the hawk returned. He had a few small insects in his mouth. He used his talon to move away the bark and dropped the insects off inside the sparrow's nest.

"Hi again. I brought you some insects," the hawk greeted, looking around. He spotted the improvements the sparrow had made to her nest and uttered, "I love what you did to the place!"

The sparrow was surprised, *"What is the deal with this hawk? Is he trying to fatten me up? Are these insects poisonous or laced with sedatives?"* She wondered.

"Thank you," she said to the hawk with a look of puzzlement and dread. The hawk noticed the sparrow's demeanor and spoke,

"Oh, I see. You must think I am up to no good for being so nice to a sparrow."

The sparrow nodded in admission.

The hawk sighed and said, "I saw you in the nest by yourself the other day and thought it was unusual. This time of year, all the sparrows are nesting. It's not common to see a single sparrow in an empty nest in spring. I figured something must have happened to you and your family."

"So, are you a grief counselor or something?" the sparrow questioned the hawk, not recognizing how sarcastic she sounded.

The hawk replied, "No, not at all. I have no training whatsoever and I am unqualified to give anyone advice,"

The hawk lowered his eyes, let out a sigh, and continued,

"It's just that I, too, lost my family last summer. A poacher found my nest and took my mate and all my babies."

The sparrow saw a glimpse of sadness in the hawk's eyes. She felt bad that she had presumed he was malicious. The sparrow said, "I am so very sorry. I mean, for your loss and my prejudice against you."

The hawk assured her that it was alright. They continued talking. As they talked, they shared the stories of their families and their losses. Recounting the traumatic experiences made the sparrow very sad, but it also made her feel different. The weight of her misery seemed to let up a little. The pain was still there, but something new also developed, and somehow that made the pain more bearable. Perhaps it was the joyful memories she recalled, or perhaps it was the knowledge that she once was loved.

The sparrow also listened intently to the hawk's story. The hawk told her how he had tried to defend the nest and his family but was not successful. The hawk told her how he had blamed himself, how angry he was at the world, how he stumbled through the dark passages of grief, how he found the light on the other side, and how he finally found himself again.

The sparrow and the hawk talked for a long time and offered each other comfort. If anyone had passed by, they would have witnessed a strange sight - a prey and a predator deeply immersed in their compassion for each other - the compassion that was just enough to keep each of them afloat until a new way forward revealed itself.

Before they said goodbye, the sparrow assured the hawk that she would be alright and that she knew the hawk would be alright too. The hawk said goodbye and flew off.

It was nighttime by then. The sparrow went inside her nest and rested. Watching the distant stars in the dark, she looked forward to starting a new day when the morning light returned.

The End

All beings, big or small, predators or prey, are subjected to suffering and heartbreaks. Compassion is what we feel when we understand the suffering others are going through. Compassion is not about finding solutions or eliminating bad feelings. It is about showing all the love and support you can - the love and support that might just give someone enough illumination in the dark tunnel of suffering, until they emerge into the light at the end of it.

SPELLBOUND

Once upon a time, there was a kingdom. The king and the queen just had a baby girl. The whole kingdom rejoiced and celebrated the birth of the princess. It was a happy time.

Deep in the forest, there lived an evil witch. No one knew exactly how old she was, but she'd lived alone in the forest for a long time. Centuries of evil deeds left her with no friends and no help. Every house chore became a hassle. She needed someone to keep her company and help around the house. The witch heard about the newborn princess and decided that the princess would make the perfect companion.

One night when there was no moon in the sky and all the stars were covered by dark clouds, the witch entered the castle. She cast a spell and put everyone to sleep, then went to the nursery and left the castle with the young princess.

The king ordered a countrywide search. All the soldiers spread out to all corners of every town in the kingdom. Unfortunately, the witch hid her deep in the forest and the young princess could not be found.

The princess grew up in captivity. The witch showed her little kindness. She made the princess do all the chores. Every year on the princess's birthday, the witch would tell her the story of her kidnap just to taunt her and remind her that she was the witch's property.

The witch taught the princess small things. The one subject the princess was naturally good at was how to talk to animals. The witch also allowed the princess to travel to town from time to time, but that was only because the witch put a spell on the princess so any human who looked at her would only see an old, repulsive woman instead of a young princess. The spell would break if the witch reversed it, or if the princess won the heart of a man who could overlook the spell and see her for who she truly was.

One of the princess's chores was to go to the farmer's market to sell fruits and vegetables from the witch's garden. Because of the spell, the townspeople only saw an old hideous woman calling for people to buy her produce. No one knew the old woman was in fact, a beautiful princess. The princess tried asking the townspeople to help her escape the witch. But when she tried talking to someone, all they saw was a hideous old hag, and no one wanted to hear what she had to say.

Years passed and the princess's regal beauty grew. And as the princess became older, the witch was meaner to her. The princess felt she needed to escape sooner than later. One day, while the princess was tending to her fruit stand in town, a handsome prince rode his horse through the farmer's market.

The princess thought, *"It is now or never,"* then she ran after the prince and yelled, "Your highness. Wait. Please. Your highness."

The prince turned around to see an old ugly woman running after him. He was repulsed by her looks. "What is it that you want?" he asked.

The princess thought quickly and said, "I was wondering if your highness would like a servant. I'd be honored to serve you."

The prince was traveling with just his horse. It would take several more days before he reached his home kingdom. Having a servant would make the trip easier. "All right. You may travel with me as my servant," he spoke.

The princess followed the prince and his horse. Not being human, the horse saw the princess for who she really was. The princess told the horse the truth about her identity. The horse felt very sorry for the princess and promised to help her.

Three days before the prince would reach his home kingdom, the horse pretended to be ill and refused to walk any further. The prince had no choice but to wait. They found an abandoned cottage. To pass the time, the prince started talking to the princess whom he saw as a hideous old hag. Even though her appearance was abhorrent, the prince found that he and the old hag had much in common. There was something endearing about the way the old woman carried herself. She was funny, sophisticated, and knowledgeable, nothing at all like her appearance would suggest.

The princess found the prince to be a true gentleman. He treated her with respect and kindness, almost as if he could see through her unappealing exterior.

After a few days, they got back on track and headed toward the prince's kingdom. It just so happened that the witch was looking for the princess and was traveling on the same road.

Ahead of her, the witch saw the prince's traveling party but did not recognize the princess. The witch decided to approach them and picked up her pace.

The princess saw the witch approaching from behind and ran into the forest to hide. The prince cried out after her,

"Hey! Where are you going? I thought we'd be together," He felt a little twinge in his heart when he thought of the possibility that the old woman might not return.

Then he turned around and saw the witch approaching. He drew out his sword, ready to fight.

The witch saw the sharp blade of the sword. She pretended to be scared, then let out a terrifying laugh,

"Oh pa-leease! Your sword is no match for my dark magic!" She then cast a spell on the prince and turned him into a rabbit.

"How do you like that now, your highness?" the witch mocked, then she laughed and laughed. When she was able to catch her breath, she said,

"You will stay a rabbit forever if you don't eat the snow lotus from the Himalayas within three days. Oh, and by the way, only I have the snow lotus and you will never find it. Goodbye, hoppy."

The witch cackled, then she walked away, very pleased with herself.

The prince felt hopeless. Who would be able to fetch the snow lotus from the Himalayas in three days? As he was hopping around, he heard the galloping noise of his horse. Someone was on the horse's back. It was the princess!

"You came back!" the prince cried out. He didn't quite like his bunny voice but the twinge in his heart was gone.

Because he was now a rabbit and not a human, the prince could see the princess in her true form. "Is this how you really look like?" he asked.

The princess told the prince everything that had happened - how she was kidnapped and enslaved and how the witch used dark magic to conceal her true appearance.

Now they had to figure out how to break the prince's spell in three days. From years of living with the witch, the princess had learned many things about exotic plants and strange ingredients. Because it's quite an inconvenience to climb up the Himalayas to pick the rare flower every winter, the witch always hid a snow lotus in her house.

"Don't worry. I will be back with the lotus in three days," she told the prince.

She put him in the cottage they'd found, made sure he had enough food and water, then got on the horse and rode off. The princess arrived at the witch's house and quietly got off the horse. She knew the witch would first make sure the lotus she kept hidden was safe, so she waited outside and observed the witch through the window. As expected, the witch took out a box from under the fireplace. She opened the box, and the snow lotus was shining bright inside. In the box next to the lotus was a bottle of potion.

As the witch was looking around, deciding where to hide the box, she heard some noise outside. She put the box down and stepped out to investigate.

The noise the witch heard was created by the horse to distract the witch. With the witch gone, the princess entered the house in the back and grab the box with the lotus and a bottle of potion. Then she heard a little voice.

"Princess! Over here!" The voice came from under the table. It was a tiny mouse.

"Dear princess, the potion in the box is very powerful. You can use it to destroy the witch. Throw the potion at her as she is about to cast a spell and the witch will be gone forever!"

The princess thanked the tiny mouse who instantly disappeared into the wall of the house.

It was not long until the witch realized there was no one outside. She came rushing inside the house to find the princess holding the snow lotus. The witch then said,

"You know, you can use the snow lotus to break the spell I put on you too. The problem is there's only one lotus and it can only break one spell. Who is it going to be for? For you or for the bunny? My oh my, I love creating dilemmas," the witch said.

The princess clutched the lotus in her hand and said, "I will bring to lotus back to the prince. I don't care if I am still under your spell. In fact, I don't even care if you turn me into an old hag permanently." One of the princess's hands was behind her back, slowly uncorking the potion.

The witch cackled loudly, "What sacrifice! If that's what you want, I am always happy to oblige!" Then the witch got ready to cast the spell to turn the princess into an old hag forever. Quickly, the princess threw the potion at the witch. As the potion touched her skin, the witch started withering away. She howled and writhed in pain. She continued moaning as she wilted into dust.

The princess put the lotus in her satchel and got on the horse. She made her way back to the prince just before the three days were over. She peeled the petals off the lotus and fed them to the bunny prince.

The rabbit turned back to the prince. Back to being human, the prince now saw the princess as an old hag again. Nonetheless, this did not diminish the gratitude and love he had for her.

The prince got on his knee. "My heart no longer belongs to me. I have seen who you are through everything we've been through, and I am giving you my heart completely," the prince said, blushing.

And just like that, the princess's spell was broken. The prince no longer saw an old hag when he looked at her. They were both ecstatic. The three of them headed off toward the princess's kingdom.

The king and the queen were overjoyed when they saw their long-lost daughter. There were endless celebrations in the kingdom. The king and the queen got to know the prince. They thought he was a fine young man. The princess and the prince got married, and the two kingdoms celebrated with them. After each of them inherited the throne from their respective parents, they merged the two kingdoms into one prosperous nation.

And they lived peacefully ever after.

The End

Often, we make assumptions based on what we see. An assumption is like a spell that prevents us from opening our minds to all the truths. Be mindful, shield yourself from the spell of assumption, lead with kindness, and navigate the world with an open heart.

MY AUNTIE QI

In the heavenly realm, there lived four fairies. The fairies were sisters. They were created by the Jade Emperor, the supreme god of the heavenly realm. When the Jade Emperor created the sisters, he gave each of them a special gift. Ta, the oldest sister could inspire kindness in anyone, even the most ruthless criminal. The second sister, Ru, could make anyone feel the suffering of others, and as a result, create compassion. The third sister, Jo, could motivate people to feel joy for others' fortunes and successes, hence promoting harmony. The youngest of the sisters was Qi. She had the gift of balance. The four sisters often traveled together to the earthly realm to help humans. Wherever they went, they inspired and motivated people to be kind and good to one another. Together, they softened the cruelest of minds and brought peace to conflicts. People praised Ta,

Ru, and Jo constantly. Not a lot of people recognized Qi. They felt that her gift was subtle and not as impactful as her sisters'.

One day, the Jade Emperor sent for the sisters. When they appeared in front of him, the Jade Emperor said to them,

"Heavenly sisters, I am very pleased with what you have done for mankind over thousands of years. But I am afraid there's one special case that needs your urgent attention."

The Jade Emperor waved his hand and a life-like image of a palace appeared. In the palace, there was a young teenage boy dressed in a regal gown.

"This is the crown prince. He is destined to be the greatest ruler the human world will ever see. Unfortunately, the boy has no proper guidance. He's surrounded by people who give him whatever he wants. None of them bothers to teach him what's right and what's wrong. I want each of you to go down to earth and be the crown prince's moral chaperon."

Ta, the fairy of kindness, was the first to volunteer. She went down to earth and followed the crown prince. Everywhere he went, Ta inspired him to have lovingkindness. The prince showed kindness to everyone he met. This started off very well. But over time, the prince began to get too attached and became sentimental easily. He would break down and cry when his kindness was not acknowledged or reciprocated. After a while, the Jade Emperor asked Ta to return to the heavens.

Ru, the fairy of compassion, was the next to go. She went down to earth and started inspiring the prince to have compassion. At first, the prince related well to other people's suffering and learned much from it. However, after a while, the compassion grew into despair. He was burdened by other people's suffering and was sad all the time. The Jade Emperor saw this and summoned Ru to return to the heavens.

Jo, the fairy of shared joy, went down to earth next. She inspired the prince to develop happiness for others around him. The prince had a strong start. He genuinely congratulated his classmates when they academically performed better than he did. He felt joy for his siblings when his father the emperor complimented them. After a while, though, the prince could not help but compare himself to his peers and this made him feel inadequate and miserable. When Jo tried to hold back her influence, the prince developed jealousy and could not bring himself to be happy for others. It wasn't long before Jo was called back to the heavens by the Jade Emperor.

This left Qi as the last fairy to finish the task. She went down to earth and decided to take a human form for the assignment. She entered the palace and transformed into an old nanny. Everyone called her Auntie Qi.

Auntie Qi's job was to bring the prince afternoon tea. She would sit with the prince and tell him stories while the prince enjoyed his afternoon treats. One afternoon, she told him the story of two wealthy men who were brothers. They lived next to each other. One day a homeless man came to the neighborhood. The wealthy older brother felt bad for the homeless man and took him in. He gave the homeless man food and offered him a place to clean up and stay for the night. The wealthy younger brother observed this and wanted to do nice things for the homeless man as well. But his intentions were different. He only wanted to treat the homeless man well so he would feel good about himself. The younger brother took the homeless man into his house the following day and gave him rounds and rounds of food and drinks. He invited everyone in the neighborhood to bear witness to his generosity. The older brother was not pleased about this. Taking in the homeless man was his idea! His! He thought of it first! And now his little brother got all the admiration. From then on, the older brother made a point to hang on to the homeless man. When his younger brother offered to do something nice for the homeless man, he would up the ante so the homeless man would choose to come to his house instead.

After a few days of going back and forth between the two wealthy men's homes, the homeless man felt it was time for him to move on. Although both brothers had been good to him, the homeless man missed his freedom. The younger brother had no problem letting the homeless man go because it was pity, not compassion, that he felt for the man. The older brother, on the other hand, had a hard time letting go of the homeless man for he had grown attached to him. He begged the homeless man not to go. When the homeless man finally left, the older wealthy brother was very sad. He stopped eating and got very ill.

Auntie Qi stopped her story and asked if the prince wanted more tea and pastry. The prince told her no. His thoughts about the story still lingered.

"What happened to the older brother in the end?" the prince asked.

"He recovered and got on with his life, your highness," answered Auntie Qi.

"They aren't really good people, the two brothers in the story," the prince observed.

Auntie Qi smiled and said, "Auntie Qi is slow. Would your highness enlighten me?"

"They may appear to be kind and compassionate. But the older one was overdoing it, and the younger one just pretended to be kind to serve his selfish purposes," the prince said.

Auntie Qi bowed to the prince and said, "Your highness is so wise. Kindness and compassion are both good virtues, but like everything in life, they must be in balance – not too much and not too little."

The following day, Auntie Qi brought the afternoon tea to the prince's chamber. She told him another story while he was sipping the tea and snacking on the rice cakes.

A woman was walking through the market with her young daughter. As she was browsing through various stalls and chatting with the vendors, her daughter wandered away. After a while, the woman noticed that her daughter was no longer beside her. She started looking for her frantically. Then she heard a big splashing sound coming from a nearby river. The woman ran as fast as she could toward the river and found her daughter struggling in the water. Neither the woman nor her daughter knew how to swim. The woman yelled out for help. Then a monk walked by. The woman ran to the monk and begged him to save her daughter. The monk told the woman that he did not know how to swim. By this time, a few more people heard the commotion and came over. The people harshly scolded the monk for not helping the poor woman. Then the woman got frustrated and jumped into the water to save her child. Now both the woman and her child were drowning. The monk looked around and found a bamboo tree. He cut down a few bamboo stems and quickly tied them together. He threw the bundled bamboo into the water and told the woman and her daughter to grab a hold of the floating bamboo. The monk pulled them both ashore, and the mother and the child were saved.

The prince finished his snacks soon as the story ended. After he wiped his mouth with a napkin, the prince said to Auntie Qi,

"The woman in the story - she makes things worse by acting impulsively. And the onlookers are so critical of the monk. They presume he does not want to help but he is the true hero."

Auntie Qi said as she was putting the afternoon tea and snacks away, "Your highness is correct. A mother's instinct is to save her child. But without thoughtfulness, she puts them both in danger. The monk, on the other hand, pauses mindfully, stays balanced despite criticism, and acts wisely."

The prince nodded in agreement. Auntie Qi excused herself and left the prince's chamber.

The next day, Auntie Qi arrived with the prince's afternoon tea. The prince was delighted to see her. He had come to enjoy her afternoon stories. He wondered what story Auntie Qi was going to tell him today.

Auntie Qi greeted the crown prince, then set the table for the afternoon tea. When the prince took a seat at the table and started his cup of tea, Auntie Qi began her story.

Many, many years ago, the Qin and the Zhao kingdoms were at war. In Zhao's country, there lived a doctor. The doctor was famous for his medical knowledge and skills. Everyone admired him but the doctor remained humbled. Whenever people mentioned his fortunes, the doctor often responded, "The eight winds cannot tear down the sky." One day, the Qin army invaded the doctor's hometown, and he was separated from his family. The doctor was eventually captured by the Qin army. The Qin put the doctor in prison with other prisoners of war. The other prisoners knew that the doctor was well respected in his homeland. They felt bad about his misfortune. But the doctor was not overly dejected. All he said was, "The eight winds cannot tear down the sky". He went on with his life just like the other prisoners. A few weeks passed and all the prisoners received news that Zhao's kingdom had fallen. The doctor's home in Zhao was burned down and no one knew what happened to his family. The other prisoners were sad and enraged by the news, but the doctor stayed composed. Again, he said, "The eight winds cannot tear down the sky."

Another few weeks passed, and news spread that the Qin's queen had fallen ill. No doctors in the Qin's kingdom could figure out how to cure her illness. The doctor heard about the queen's symptoms and knew right away how to help. He asked the guards to allow him to see the queen. At first, the prison guards ignored him, but after several days, the queen's health got worse. Out of desperation, the guards told the doctor he would be granted permission to see the queen in the morning. The other Zhao prisoners thought this was a good opportunity to avenge their homeland. They told the doctor to use poison instead of medicine on the queen. They reminded him that the Qin destroyed his home and separated him from his family. But the only thing the doctor said was, "The eight winds cannot tear down the sky."

In the morning the guards brought the doctor to see the Qin's king. The king was skeptical. He knew the doctor was famous and highly skilled, but he was from Zhao, and the Qin and the Zhao were enemies. Who's to say the doctor wouldn't intentionally make the queen worse to take vengeance? So, the king said, "If you can restore the queen's health, I will set you free. But if the queen gets worse, I will take your life."

Then the guards let the doctor to the queen's chamber. The doctor examined her and quickly figured out what the problem was. He wrote down a prescription and handed it to the chambermaid. He told her to get all the herbal ingredients on the prescription as fast as she possibly could. When the chambermaid returned, the doctor mixed the herbs and gave the mixture to the queen. The queen's health improved quickly. The Qin king kept his promise and released the doctor. He moved back to his hometown in Zhao and rebuilt the house. He looked for his family but did not find them.

Auntie Qi stopped the story, and the prince said, "How sad. He did not find his family."

Auntie Qi looked at the prince and said, "How kind of your highness to have compassion for the doctor. But we know the doctor will be alright because —"

"The eight winds cannot tear down the sky!" the prince said.

Auntie Qi bowed slightly and said, "Your highness is, once again, correct. There are eight winds in this world – loss and gain, praise and blame, pleasure and pain, and fame and disrepute. These winds constantly pass through everyone's life. If we allow our minds to falter every time the winds come, we will be carried away in all directions and won't have peace of mind or a clear focus in life. A great mind is like the sky. It allows winds, clouds, stars, the sun, and the moon to pass, yet it remains unshakable and open."

Auntie Qi recognized that the young prince had learned enough valuable lessons and it was time to reveal herself. She transformed herself back into the divine form. The prince was bewildered. Qi's three sisters appeared alongside her. They all greeted the prince and introduced themselves. Then Qi addressed the prince,

"Each of my sisters has inspired your highness to have lovingkindness, compassion, and sympathetic joy. I, myself, represent equanimity. Equanimity is a perfectly balanced, unwavering presence of mind – just like the sky not being swayed by the eight winds. Without equanimity, kindness turns into clinginess, compassion becomes pity, and sympathetic joy leads to unhelpful comparison. When mindfulness is seated in equanimity, it leads to wise and helpful actions."

The prince respectfully bowed to Qi. Then Qi continued,

"I bid your highness farewell. It has been a pleasure and privilege to share my wisdom with your highness. I do not doubt that you will become a great ruler. My sisters and I will be watching over you from the heavens."

Then the four fairies floated up in the sky. The prince was still amazed by all that had happened. When the fairies were out of sight, he went to his desk and started writing everything Auntie Qi had ever taught him. He put all the pages together into a book. On the cover of the book, he wrote, "My Auntie Qi". The prince studied Qi's teachings daily. And just like the Jade Emperor had prophesized, the prince grew up to be one of the greatest rulers the human world had ever known.

The End

The four divine qualities in Buddhism are lovingkindness, compassion, sympathetic joy, and equanimity. These qualities are not rare gifts that some are born with, and others lack. They are inborn transcendent qualities we all have. Get to know your divine qualities and nurture them. Maintain them in balance. You can be the sublime presence in the lives of everyone around you, including your own.

THE MERCHANT AND THE DONKEY

Once upon a time, in a foreign land, there lived a merchant. The merchant owned a small shop in town and a donkey. The shop had all sorts of knick-knacks and trinkets one could imagine. Every week the merchant would take the donkey to the city and trade goods with other merchants. The donkey would carry the traded goods back to the shop. This went on without interruption. It was enough to earn a living and the merchant had a comfortable life.

The merchant's shop was located in a large marketplace. Next to his shop, there was a much bigger shop owned by a wealthy businessman. In the businessman's shop, there were nicer, grander, more expensive inventories. The businessman also owned a beautiful horse that always stood elegantly in front of his shop.

The merchant always watched the businessman with envy. He wanted a bigger store and a horse, but all he had was a small shop and a donkey. The donkey, though sensed that it was a disappointment to the merchant, remained loyal and diligent with his work.

One day, a traveling caravan passed through the marketplace. One of the caravanners was walking an absolutely gorgeous horse alongside his cart. The caravanner was yelling,

"Horse for sale or trade. Horse for sale or trade."

This immediately caught the merchant's attention. He rushed out of his shop and approached the caravanner.

"How much is the horse?" the merchant asked enthusiastically.

The caravanner glanced at him. He instantly recognized the merchant's eager interest in the horse. The caravanner knew he could hike up the price and the merchant would pay anything for the horse.

"Everything you own in the shop," the caravanner said with a confident smile.

The merchant thought of the proposal, *"Everything in my shop? I'd be starting over from scratch afterward. But with the horse, I could get more goods to fill the store. Maybe this is a good investment."* He continued reasoning with himself.

As he was calculating in his mind, the merchant saw his donkey and had an idea.

"Would you trade the horse for my donkey? He's very strong and can endure any kind of weather. He's not afraid of thunder. He even pulled a cart through a rainstorm once, nonstop!" the merchant tried advertising his donkey.

"That donkey??" asked the caravanner, "you mean, *that* donkey for *this* horse?" the caravanner repeated, then he let out a hysterical laugh, "that is so funny. You are killing me!"

The merchant got embarrassed. Other storekeepers and townspeople were now paying attention to their conversation. The merchant wanted to end this transaction quickly, so he said, "All right, all right. That's fine if you don't want my donkey. You can have everything in my shop for that horse. Is that still a deal?"

The caravanner wiped off his tears from laughing and said, "Of course. I'll take everything in the shop. You can have this horse. Oh, and please keep that donkey. I don't want it."

The caravanner continued to laugh as he loaded all the merchant's goods in his caravan. When he was finished, he handed over the horse to the merchant. The merchant was now a horse owner! He couldn't be prouder. He paraded the horse around the marketplace. He loved hearing the "oohs" and "aahs" people let out when they saw his gorgeous horse. The donkey, on the other hand, was left tied to the post in front of the merchant's bare store with a sad look on its face.

The merchant had to start over and find merchandise to put in his empty store. He decided to go to a faraway city with his new horse and a carriage. He left the donkey behind. He asked the businessman next door to give the donkey water and whatever scraps of food the businessman could find.

The merchant took off with the horse. The road was rough, and the terrain was not easy to navigate. The horse had to stop often for water and rest. Sometimes the horse refused to walk at all. After several days, the merchant did not get any closer to the city. Food and water were running low. The merchant got desperate and thought he might have to return empty-handed.

That night, a big storm came. The rain poured down from the sky continuously. Deafening thunders roared every few minutes. The merchant and his horse took shelter in the forest. The horse looked more and more nervous with each thundering. Then suddenly, after a very loud rumble, the horse got spooked and ran away.

The merchant was left by himself and a carriage. "What am I going to do now? I can't pull this carriage by myself anywhere. I won't make it to the city. I am ruined." He thought to himself, imagining the worst. Then he began to cry.

Back at his shop, the rainstorm was also passing by. The donkey heard the sound of thunder from afar. The donkey got restless. It paced back and forth but could not get very far because it was tied to a post. After much determination, the donkey kicked down the post and freed itself. It ran off in the direction of the thunder.

The merchant was crying in despair when he saw a shadow approaching. He looked up and saw his loyal donkey. The merchant cried even harder, but this time with joy and gratitude. He hitched the carriage to the donkey, and the two of them forged ahead on the road toward the city.

The rain went on all night. But the merchant and the donkey kept on with their mission. The road condition was difficult. And at one point, the merchant wanted to give up and stop. The donkey, on the other hand, known for stubbornness, wouldn't let him.

By the morning, they arrived at the faraway city's main marketplace. The merchant spent the day making profitable trades. He loaded new purchases onto the carriage. And he and the donkey began their journey home.

The homeward trip was faster. Unlike the horse, the donkey could travel a long distance without water, and they did not have to make frequent stops.

Along the way, the merchant found his runaway horse prancing elegantly in an open field. He lured it over with an apple, then grabbed it by the rein. Then all three of them were homebound.

When the merchant arrived at his shop, he unloaded the carriage and put new items on the shelves and display tables. He gave the donkey and the horse food and water, then took a well-deserved rest.

In the morning, the merchant put up a banner that read "grand re-opening" above the shop. The grand re-opening was a success from the start. By the end of the day, the merchant turned a huge profit. As he was closing the shop, so was the businessman next door.

WAKE

The businessman said to the merchant, "What a good day for business. Your shop attracted so many people and they stopped by my shop to look and buy stuff as well. Thanks to your grand re-opening!"

"Indeed. I am glad I went to the faraway city to get the uncommon goods. The customers kept coming to buy exotic things they never saw before," the merchant replied.

"Splendid!" the businessman said, "did you sell everything in your shop?" he asked.

The merchant thought for a moment, "Not everything," the merchant said, "there's one thing left in my shop that you might be interested in. Would you like to buy my horse?"

"Your new horse? The one you traded everything for?" the businessman asked with a surprised look.

"Yes, the horse I lost almost everything for. It is a beautiful horse, but I found out it's not for me. It turns out everything I need already belongs to me," the merchant said, looking at the donkey.

The businessman chuckled and said, "As you know, I am a horse fancier. I will pay you handsomely for this beauty."

The merchant sold his horse. He used the money to buy high-quality barley straw, sugar beet, carrots, and pears for the donkey. The donkey worked faithfully for the merchant for many years. When the time came for it to retire, the merchant built it a sanctuary. And it lived there peacefully until the end of its days.

The End

> *When we want something and do not get it, we will often discover later that the very something is not what we really need after all.*
>
> *When you love what you have, you will have everything you need. And when you focus on what you lack, you will never feel enough. There's magic in gratitude. It instantly turns lack into abundance*

TRUE LOVE

Once upon a time, there was a kingdom that was
ruled by a young king and his queen. They were a
wonderful match. The king was handsome and brave.
The queen was intelligent and kind. Despite their youth,
they ruled the land wisely and the young couple was
adored by all the citizens.

The king and queen were happy together for a few
years. Then the young king was struck by an illness. The
king was so frail that the queen had to rule the country
on his behalf. When she was not tied up with governing,
the queen devoted as much time as she could to her
husband. She consulted with all the physicians in the
kingdom to find a cure for the king's sickness. She went
to the temple daily to pray to all the gods to heal the

king. She became a strict vegan in hopes that doing so would please the gods. Sadly, nothing worked. And after years of declining health, the king succumbed to his illness and passed away.

The whole kingdom mourned the loss of the great king. Because the late king was so revered and loved, all the citizens chose to wear black in mourning. And the whole country held no celebrations of any sort for the entire year.

After a year, normal life slowly resumed for the citizens. The same, however, could not be said about the queen. No matter how much time had passed, there was still a big void in her that could not be filled. The queen continued to go over official business competently. But she kept to herself and stayed inside the castle. She continued wearing black and kept with her vegan diet.

The royal advisor and court officials were worried about the queen. They thought her grief was morose. They all believed she needed to find herself a new love and start getting on with her life.

"It's been a while. Shouldn't she be over it already?" they would say about the queen behind her back.

The queen's royal advisor was one of the people who wanted the queen to find a new love and be happy. He did not have the courage to suggest that to her directly. After much discussion with other officials, the royal advisor concocted a plan.

The advisor knew a witch who dwelled in the dark forest outside town. The witch was powerful though peculiar. The advisor traveled to the dark forest and found the witch's hut. The witch answered the door and welcomed the advisor inside. Then they talked about the advisor's plan. Before the advisor left, the witch gave him a bottle of potion and whispered instructions in his ear.

Two weeks after the advisor met with the witch, the queen started feeling unwell. The queen felt tired all the time and her vision deteriorated. She was only able to see things in black and white. The queen's doctor was at a loss about what was ailing the queen. The royal advisor then suggested that dark magic must have been responsible for the queen's condition. He convinced the queen to have a consultation with the witch. The queen eventually agreed, and the witch was summoned.

"Greetings, your majesty," the witch said, she looked visibly anxious when she saw the queen.

The advisor asked the witch whether the queen was under some dark magic. The witch looked at the advisor, then at the queen. When the advisor repeated the question, the witch reluctantly replied, "In my humble opinion, your majesty indeed is under a gloomy spell. The good news is there's a cure."

The advisor chimed in, "That is wonderful news. Tell us what will cure her majesty's ailment. Is it true love's kiss?"

The witch appeared irritated. She turned to the advisor and said to him, "No spells in the world are broken by kisses. That only works in fairy tales."

"So true love without a kiss then?" asked the advisor, who stared intently at the witch. The witch recognized that there was a script to follow, so she sighed and said, "Fine. Sure. True love can break this gloomy spell."

The queen subtly rolled her eyes, "If that's the case then there's no hope for me. My true love died last year when we lost the king."

The queen was about to dismiss the witch when the royal advisor interjected,

"Your majesty. With all due respect, your well-being is of the utmost importance to the kingdom and all its citizens. We don't know if this spell is going to create more problems for your health if left unaddressed. The country already lost its king. We can't lose you too. Why don't we listen to this wise sorceress and see if anyone can bring you true love to break the spell?"

The queen relented. She was certain no one would be able to offer her true love. But the advisor was persistent, and she figured that was the simplest way to get him off her back. Besides, it would be nice to be able to see colors and not feel fatigued all the time.

As the royal advisor escorted the witch out, the witch was trying to tell him something. The advisor, not wanting to make a scene and cause the queen to change her mind, rushed the witch outside and declined to speak to her afterward.

News spread throughout the land that the young queen was looking for true love to cure her illness. Suitors from far and wide traveled to the queen's kingdom to try their hands. Each of them was asked to bring their proof of true love. After much contest, there were down to three prominent suitors.

An emperor from overseas crossed the ocean to meet the queen. He brought with him 100 triremes, each filled with diamonds, gold bars, and jewels. The emperor unloaded the precious materials in the queen's treasury with the promise of more riches if the queen were to choose his proof of true love.

A sultan from the land beyond the great desert arrived with a team of architects and construction workers. They built an extravagant floating park right next to the queen's palace. The park was to have 33 levels and once completed, it would have been the tallest structure in the world. In the middle of the floating park, there would be an elevator to the top, powered by horses and pulleys. One could see the entire world from the top of the structure.

A prince from the kingdom on the other side of the mountain brought with him troupes of performing artists. They set up shows and musicals to play all day and all night. The shows told classic stories of love and romance. The prince also brought a thousand poets who wrote a thousand love poems for the queen daily. The prince made the shows, musicals, and poem readings available to the public as well. Because of all the moving love stories, marriage rates tripled within the kingdom.

The queen was impressed by the wealth and extravagance the suitors had brought with them. But besides the sense of awe, nothing sentimental developed in the queen's heart. Nonetheless, the queen felt obligated to give the suitors a chance. She spent time getting to know them and invited them to dinner each night.

One day, the queen took a break from entertaining the suitors and took a walk in the palace garden by herself. As she was strolling, she saw an old woman. The old woman dressed regally. The queen thought the old woman must be a noble lady accompanying one of the suitors. The old woman stopped and admired a wall that was covered by flowering bougainvillea.

"These flowers bloom so spectacularly here," said the old woman without turning to face the queen.

The queen was a little surprised. This woman must not have known that she was in the presence of the queen. The queen decided not to reveal herself and replied to the old woman,

"The flowers are spectacular indeed. Bougainvillea does very well in the sun. This wall is south-facing and gets good sun all day in every season."

The old woman, still admiring the flowers, kept her back turned to the queen and said, "You are absolutely right! It is the sun, isn't it? When I was a little girl, I used to help my father with gardening. He taught me so much about plants and flowers."

That made the queen smile. What the old woman said reminded her of her own childhood. She used to love spending time with her father. She, too, worked in the garden with her father. He taught her how to take care of plants. Her father was a good cook, and he showed her simple dishes when she helped him in the kitchen. Her knowledge of art and calligraphy all came from him. These childhood memories warmed the queen's heart and brought her joy.

The queen was about to ask the old woman her identity, but the old woman turned around to face the queen and said matter-of-factly,

"It's too bad that the bougainvillea is going to die soon. Do you see that?" the old woman pointed to clumps of withered foliage on the corner of the wall, "root rot, perhaps?"

The queen crouched down to examine the plant. The old woman was right. The bougainvillea had root rot. The queen wanted to ask the old woman more questions, but when the queen looked up, the old woman was gone.

At the end of the day, the queen had dinner with the three suitors. The emperor talked about how he ran a tight budget to make sure there were surpluses year after year. The sultan argued that life experiences made a person richer than any treasure in the world. The prince from the land on the other side of the mountain tried distinguishing himself by speaking in poems and sonnets throughout dinner.

The queen smiled politely through the chaotic and strange dinner conversation. The whole time she was thinking about her encounter with the old woman. She thought about the things she enjoyed doing in childhood and wondered why she had stopped doing them. She thought about what the old woman said about the bougainvillea and its root rot.

The following day, the queen returned to the garden, hoping to see the old woman again. She waited by the bougainvillea wall. Toward the end of the day, the old woman appeared. When she saw the queen, she asked,

"Did you figure out how to treat the bougainvillea?"

The queen shook her head. She had meant to ask the palace gardener to take care of it, but she did not get around to it. The old woman continued, "Bougainvillea is very sturdy. It doesn't need a lot of care and it thrives in the worst conditions. But nothing is so hardy that it can be completely neglected," she then looked at the queen and gently asked, "would you care to help me?"

The old woman then stooped down and started digging up the soil at the base of the bougainvillea with her hands. The queen got down on her knees and helped her.

The two women dug up the sick bougainvillea and carefully removed the infected roots. As they worked together, they talked and found they had much in common. The queen avoided asking the woman specifics as she did not want to disclose the identity of her own. After they finished taking care of the plant, the old woman said to the queen cheerfully, "Now we will see how the plant will do. No matter how it turns out, it is still better than dying slowly with the root rot, right?"

The queen gave her a warm smile and nodded in agreement. She invited the woman inside for a cup of tea, but the old woman declined.

"That is kind of you, but I must get going. Shall we meet here again tomorrow to see how the bougainvillea recovers?"

The two women bid each other farewell. The queen went inside to get ready for dinner with the suitors.

That evening over dinner, the sultan gave the queen detailed updates on the construction of the floating park. The emperor boasted that he could build many more floating parks with his wealth. The prince from the land on the other side of the mountain tried making an argument that art was the most enriching thing in anyone's life. The three kept making a case for their strengths throughout the entire meal.

The queen did not pay much attention to the kerfuffle among the suitors. She was thinking about the conversation she had with the old woman. She pondered the woman's comment about the plant needing love and care despite being naturally strong and hardy. And she was wondering how the plant would do in the morning.

The next day, the queen went out in the garden early in the morning. The bougainvillea looked mostly alive, though some parts of the plant had wilted overnight. The queen found pruning scissors and started cutting off the plant's dead parts. Then she heard the old woman's voice.

"Good morning. We are both early today," the old woman greeted the queen merrily. She noticed that the queen was trimming off the parts of the plant that had become dead. The old woman said to the queen, "would you look at that? We stressed the plant by cutting off the diseased roots. Some parts died. Some survived and will regrow. Isn't life a wonder?"

The queen stayed quiet. Something the old woman said seemed very familiar and personal. The old woman noticed the change in the queen's facial expression and said to her tenderly, "I lost my husband when I was young. A big chunk of my liveliness was ripped off of me, and I never thought I'd survive the grief. But I did. I regrew just like the bougainvillea. I regrew parts of me to adapt to the new reality that didn't have my husband in it. Grief is amazing that way. It reshapes you. You must allow it to do its work. Stay grounded in your self-love while it is transforming you."

The queen looked at the old woman carefully. The face looked so familiar now. She reminded her of someone.

"Who are you?" the queen asked.

The old woman turned to her and said with a warm smile, "This might be confusing for you, but I am you in 30 years."

The young queen took a step back. This sounded impossible. But when she looked more closely at the old woman, she saw traces of herself. The woman must have been in her 60s and she carried her age very well.

"I, I don't understand. Am I in the future or are you in the past?" the young queen asked.

The old woman laughed and said, "Thirty years ago, I was where you are now, talking to a strange older woman who claimed to be me from the future. I found it very hard to believe her then, just like how you feel about me now. I am going to tell you the same thing my future self told me 30 years ago. Are you ready for it?"

The queen nodded slowly. She was both curious and apprehensive of what her future self was about to tell her.

The old woman grabbed the young queen by the shoulders and said to her lovingly, "You are extraordinary, and I am very proud of you. There's no way you can disappoint me. No matter how bad things get, I will never leave you. I will always take care of you. And I love you very, very much."

Then the old woman pulled her into an embrace. She then turned around and walked away. The young queen remained in the garden by herself for a while.

When the queen went back inside the palace, she instructed the royal dresser to add colorful clothes to her wardrobe. She ordered the kitchen to stop making her vegan foods.

A few days passed and the queen asked the three suitors for an audience. As all the suitors were seated in the throne hall, the queen entered and addressed the suitors,

"Most distinguished gentlemen, I am overwhelmed with gratitude that you are all here. You chose to come to my kingdom with a promise of true love. You have all brought an extraordinary display of grandeur, and it is all so spectacular. I wanted to share the wonderful news with all of you. My illness is completely cured. I can see everything in vibrant colors, and I no longer feel fatigued all the time,"

All the suitors looked at each other. The advisor and other royal officials were all amazed by the announcement. The queen continued speaking,

"During your visit, I've learned so much about wealth, the world, and the arts. But most importantly, I learned about true love. I, for one, used to think my one true love was over after my husband's death. But I was wrong. He was my great love, but the truest, most unconditional, most faithful love I will ever have, is with myself. It took me some time to allow myself to accept that. And that's what has cured my illness."

It became clear to all the suitors that none of them had anything to do with the queen's recovery. They congratulated the queen on her good health. Soon after, each said farewell to the queen and left the kingdom.

The kingdom rejoiced at the news of the queen's good health. The queen's reign was long and prosperous. She became one of the greatest rulers the kingdom had ever seen.

The End

Epilogue

The news of the queen's recovery from the gloomy spell spread like wildfire. The witch heard the news and rushed to the palace. She demanded to speak to the royal advisor in private.

When they were both by themselves, the royal advisor said to the witch excitedly, "Our plan worked out splendidly, don't you think?"

"What plan? That was not *the* plan! And that's why I am here," the witch said.

"What are you talking about? The queen felt ill because of the spell and the true love she had for herself cured her," the advisor argued.

The witch looked exasperated and asked the advisor, "How did you give the queen the potion?"

"I put it in her broth, of course. That's what you told me," the advisor said.

"You fool! I said put it in her bath! Not broth!" the witch said, she was getting increasingly agitated.

The advisor gasped audibly. Then they got into a fierce debate about whether the mistake was because of the advisor's poor hearing or due to the witch's missing teeth. When they realized it was probably the combination of the two, the witch spoke in the most irritated tone.

"When you asked me to go to the palace to meet the queen, I knew right away she didn't get the potion. The real potion was supposed to turn her skin black-and-white, not make her see things in black and white. Her being colorblind had nothing to do with my potion. That's just vitamin A deficiency, plain and simple! She probably missed a few other vitamins as well, being a vegan for so long. Her vision improved after she had enough food with Vitamin A. True love had nothing to do with any of it. I tried to tell you about this that day, but you kept shoving me out the door and didn't want to listen!"

The advisor's jaw dropped. Then he thought of something, "What about the mysterious old woman from the future? That's got to be some magic, right?" the advisor asked hopefully.

The witch said, "I hate to break it to you, but vitamin B12 deficiency can cause hallucination. We just got lucky that the queen got the good kind of hallucination that worked in our favor. Can you imagine if she had gone 'queen of hearts' on all of us?"

"This is unbelievable. Should we tell her majesty the truth?" the advisor asked.

The witch threw her hands in the air and told the advisor she wanted no part of it. The witch instructed him not to contact her in the future.

"One thing for sure, life is stranger than fairy tales," the witch concluded.

The one person you will spend every single minute of the rest of your life with is yourself. Your body is the dwelling place of the greatest love. It is your companion and your friend. Treat it well with love, kindness, and respect.

And take your vitamins.

BOSSY BETHANY

Deep in the redwoods, there was a village of Sasquatches hidden far in the forest. The village was so remote that no humans ever knew of its existence. Sasquatches were intelligent and peaceful creatures and the villagers lived in harmony.

In the village lived a young Sasquatch named Moon. Moon lived by himself in a beautiful house. He worked as a pharmacist at an apothecary in town. He liked his job and the people he worked with. Life was good.

That was until one day when Moon noticed strange things at night. It started one evening when he was awakened by a whisper next to his ear. The whisper asked,

"Did you give Mrs. Spruce the right medication today?"

Moon got up and looked around the room. There was no one. Then he thought of what the voice said. He recounted the meeting with Mrs. Spruce earlier in the day. Moon felt certain he had given her the right medication. He tried going back to sleep but ended up tossing and turning for the rest of the night.

In the morning, Moon rushed to the apothecary and looked over the records. He did give Mrs. Spruce the right medication in the right amount. Moon was relieved.

The following night, he was startled by the whisper. Again, it questioned him about what he had done that day.

"You shouldn't have given Mr. Sky that advice. He did not appreciate it. You should have just minded your own business."

Moon woke up and turned on the light. He looked for the source of the whisper. There was no one else in the room. Earlier that day, Mr. Sky had picked up his medication for acid reflux. Moon had told him not to eat too late at night so he wouldn't have reflux symptoms. Mr. Sky rolled his eyes at him, but at the time Moon thought the advice was professionally sound and appropriate, and he didn't think much of it. Now that the voice questioned it, Moon started thinking perhaps he shouldn't have said anything.

He got out of bed and explored all the rooms. No one else was there. Was there a ghost in his house? He kept the lights on all night and did not go back to sleep.

The apothecary Moon worked at was owned by a Sasquatch named River. River and Moon had become good friends since Moon started working there. Moon told River about the ghost voice he'd been hearing at night.

"A ghost?" River asked, "I think you are imagining things."

Moon told River that the voice sounded very real, and he didn't think things up. Moon assumed River did not believe him and did not mention the voice to River again.

The voice continued to visit. At first, it only happened at night and Moon was afraid to sleep. Unfortunately, over time, the whisper came to him when he was awake, and pretty much at all times. And it arrived more often and more intrusively.

"Remember the time you let your soccer team down by missing the penalty shot? You are such a loser," said the voice.

Moon, in fact, was a very good soccer player. His school team got to the finals of the tournament. He had scored so many goals to get the team there. But it was that one penalty shot in the finals that he missed. Moon felt terrible about the missed shot back then. He thought he had forgotten about that experience. Now that the voice brought it up again, Moon felt very bad about himself.

As time went on, the voice not only brought up past mistakes but also gave him grim warnings of what was to come.

"If you don't get enough sleep tonight, you are going to be so tired in the morning. Then you will make a mistake. People will get hurt."

The voice sounded rational on the surface. Yes, Moon would feel a little tired without enough sleep, but the bleak consequences the voice predicted only added to Moon's anxiety. And he could not go to sleep at all at night. He felt tired all the time. When Moon was at work, he went over everything many times in fear of making mistakes. He thought being more thorough would lessen his anxiety, but more obsessive thinking did nothing but intensify his apprehension.

All of this took a toll on Moon's mental and physical health. He was often distracted and jumpy. He had sweaty palms and developed heart palpitations easily.

River noticed the changes in Moon's moods and demeanors. She asked Moon about the voice and found out things had gotten worse. She felt so bad for Moon.

"Who does the voice sound like?" River asked.

Moon had never thought of that before. He tried hard to put a name to the voice. The voice did not sound like a particular Sasquatch he knew. It was more of a combination of his older brother, a friend from high school, and an old college professor.

"Interesting," said River, "what were your common experiences with these Sasquatches?"

Moon recalled. Growing up, his older brother was a stellar student and superstar athlete. Moon looked up to him and tried very hard to be just like his brother. They had a good relationship, but deep down, he felt inadequate next to his brother. As for the high school friend, they were not very close, but they got compared to each other a lot because of their similarities. There was always a sense of competition with this friend.

"What about the college professor?" River asked.

"Oh, he was the worst!" Moon answered, "he was mean and not supportive at all. He once predicted I would never graduate. I worked harder and finished college with honors to prove him wrong."

River said, "I know who this voice is. It's your inner critic. We all have one," then River had a moment of realization and excitedly said to Moon, "let's give it a name! What do you want to call it? Is it a he- or a she-Sasquatch?"

Moon paused to think, then he thought of a name, "A she-Sasquatch? We will call her bossy Bethany?"

"I love it!" River remarked. The two laughed at themselves at the idea of bossy Bethany. The laugh made Moon feel much better. The ghost voice now had a name.

River paused from laughing and gave Moon a playful look, "Let's give her a wardrobe!" She suggested.

River grabbed a piece of paper and started drawing.
The two friends dressed up bossy Bethany in an
oversized floral muumuu. They put a large turban on her
head. They made her wear unfashionably large round

glasses and put heavy makeup on her face. The image of
bossy Bethany was so absurd, and the two friends burst
out good belly laughs.

Moon took the drawing of bossy Bethany home with him and put it up in the kitchen. That evening, when he was by himself, the voice whispered in his ear.

"By telling River about your anxiety, she thinks you are weak and pathetic, and she feels sorry for you."

For a second Moon almost believed the voice. Then he remembered that the voice had a name. He paused, took a deep breath, and said,

"Bossy Bethany, there's no way you know that."

The voice was persistent, "No one really likes you in this town. You have no other friends."

Moon took a few more deep breaths. He glanced at the drawing of bossy Bethany in her large muumuu, a turban, and round glasses. The image made him smile. He thought of what bossy Bethany said and in his better judgment, Moon said,

"Bossy Bethany, I know that's not true. Please go back to your room now."

Moon did not hear from bossy Bethany for the rest of the night. He was pleasantly surprised. The following day, he told River what had happened. River was truly happy for her friend.

From then on, when bossy Bethany started speaking, Moon would pause, take a deep breath, and pay attention to what bossy Bethany's real message was. He noticed that bossy Bethany sometimes had good intentions, though she expressed them in negative tones. With mindfulness, Moon learned to reframe and rephrase what bossy Bethany tried telling him.

So, when bossy Bethany reminded him, "Remember a few years ago, you got rejected from the school of your choice? You are not good enough!"

Moon would stay mindful and present, and rephrase it to, "The school was not the right choice for me. Not getting into that school allowed me to enter a better school, which led me to all the opportunities I have today," Moon then said to bossy Bethany, "thanks for reminding me how far I have come. Go to your room now."

Or when bossy Bethany said to Moon, "Your presentation tomorrow is extremely important. You cannot mess it up. If you fail, it will ruin your career, and you will never recover!"

Moon paused and maintained his awareness in the present. In his mindfulness, he reframed it to, "The presentation is important, and I am prepared. It is all right to be nervous. It does not have to be perfect," then he said to bossy Bethany, "thanks for your input but you can go to your room now."

The voice was no longer a mysterious phenomenon that happened outside Moon's control. It had a name and personality. And Moon knew exactly who the voice was. Bossy Bethany was the culmination of years of self-doubt, perfectionism, and fear of failure. She started off benevolently as a voice of motivation and emotional protection, but bossy Bethany quickly grew unrealistically critical and demanding. Bossy Bethany fed on ruminations of the past and false predictions of the future. As long as Moon stayed in the present and stayed mindful, bossy Bethany was not able to call the shots. Over time, bossy Bethany stayed more silent in her room. Moon was aware that bossy Bethany would always be a part of him, but he had the power to stop her and send her to her room when her opinions were not needed.

Moon lived peacefully ever after in the Sasquatch village, which, to this day, remains hidden from the rest of the world.

The End

Our inner critic grows up alongside us and knows all the nuances of our hopes, fears, passions, and insecurities. It knows exactly what button to push and when. That said, the inner critic is not an enemy. It is born as a part of our development, and we cannot banish it entirely from our minds. Stay mindfully on course and remain in the driver's seat as the kindest, most loving, most patient, and most generous version of yourself. Invite the inner critic along for the ride. There's only one rule. It is not allowed to drive!

THE PRINCE WHO BECAME BEAUTIFUL

Once upon a time, there lived a prince who ruled a small kingdom. For years, the prince tried looking for a suitable partner, but he was not successful. And as he became older, he was more and more self-conscious about his appearance. He thought he was unattractive, and his unattractiveness had everything to do with him being single. He would go on dates and spend all the time talking about how much he disliked several parts of his body. The prince's date would assure him he looked just fine, but the prince could never be convinced. At best, he would think the date was being kind. At worst, he would assume the date was patronizing him or ridiculing his looks. As a result, no one ever went on a second date with the prince.

For reasons that were not clear, the prince kept company with beautiful models and actors. Perhaps it was his need to surround himself with beauty to lift his spirit? Or perhaps he was seeking profound revelation beyond the surface of the beautiful people? Regardless of the intention, the prince would ask his entourage of gorgeous individuals what he should do to look better. And his beautiful friends would always come up with recommendations.

"You need to be more muscular," a model named Fabio suggested.

The prince was already in shape for his age. It's just that he was at an age when most men got softer around the edges even with regular exercises. But Fabio himself was flawless, and you don't get to have a name like Fabio and *not* know a thing or two about beauty.

The prince hired a personal trainer. He started a new workout regimen and began a very strict diet. After several weeks, he became more muscular, and his body fat went down to 15%. He received more attention from eligible singles. Still, he felt inadequate and could not find a person to continue dating with. The workout and diet plans soon proved unsustainable. The prince felt hungry and wretched all the time. He gave up the workout and went back to his balanced diet.

"You need to be taller," a gorgeous influencer named Kameron-Tiffany told him.

The prince was already weight-height proportionate but because Kameron-Tiffany must have known what she was talking about, the prince agreed with her. He hired a shoemaker to make him platform boots that would add at least 3 inches to his height. The prince looked taller and got more notice from other singles. But he still could not find a person to build a relationship with. After a while, the prince put away the special boots because they hurt his feet too much.

"Your nose needs to be slimmer and straighter," an actor/model named Troyes (the 's' is silent) proposed.

The prince's nose was a little crooked from a fight he had as a child. The crooked nose was very subtle, but Troyes and his silent 's' convinced the prince a new nose was urgently needed. The prince underwent a procedure, and after a few weeks of recovery, his nose looked narrower and straighter. Still, the prince could not find anyone to have consecutive dates with. Unfortunately, the new nose made it harder for him to breathe. He had to mouth-breathe most of the time, and he snored loudly at night.

Besides hanging out with models and actors, the prince enjoyed going to the library to read up on the latest fashion and beauty trends. The librarian, whose name was Jill, grew up with the prince. Jill noticed how the prince's appearance had changed over time. She wanted to tell him his looks were not the problem. But as long as he welcomed influences from the entourage of models and actors, Jill knew her words would mean very little to the prince.

One day, the prince was browsing through the latest fashion periodicals in the library. Jill stopped by his desk, and they exchanged pleasantries. She noticed that the prince looked different from when she had seen him a week before.

"This is my new look this week," explained the prince, "Troyes said it's the hottest trend in Milan right now."

The prince's look was objectively quite horrendous and age-inappropriate. Yet, Jill smiled politely, then excused herself to the back room to sort the returned books. As she was putting the returns into different bins, she noticed a book she had never seen before. The book was stuck at the bottom of the stack all the way to the very back of the shelf. It looked ancient and mystical. The title was "The Book of Beauty". Jill thought the prince might be interested and showed the book to him.

The prince examined the book with great curiosity. He asked to take it back to the castle, then he thanked Jill and left the library.

The prince arrived at his palace and started exploring the book in private. The book had two parts. Part one was titled "Formed", and part two was called "Formless". The table of content of Part One had many chapters named after different body parts: skin, eyes, nose, mouth, arms, legs, etc. At the end of each chapter, there was a blank page with tiny instructions in the footnote.

"Draw the body you love and watch it become reality."

The prince got very curious. He found the chapter about the eyes and started drawing a pair of beautiful blue eyes on the blank page at the end of the chapter.

The prince immediately rushed to the mirror to see if his eyes had changed but nothing seemed to happen. He sighed, put the book on the nightstand, and turned in for the night.

The following morning, as the prince was in the bathroom, getting ready to brush his teeth, he noticed his new pair of eyes. His eyes were intensely blue like sapphires, and they were mesmerizing. The prince jumped up and down with excitement. He ordered his page to round up all his model and actor friends to witness his beautiful eyes.

The beautiful friends arrived and were thrilled to see the prince's blazing blue eyes. The prince did not say anything about the ancient book to his beautiful friends.

After the viewing party was over and all the models and actors left, the prince went back to the book and flipped through it until he found the chapter about the mouth. At the end of the chapter, he drew luscious lips and colored them light pink and finished them with a gloss. He then went to bed, waiting for the miracle to happen in the morning.

The morning came, and the prince got his new lips – full, glossy, and luscious. He summoned his model and actor friends to the palace. They appeared excited for him at first. But shortly before the party departed, Troyes mentioned something to the prince.

"You look gorgeous with your new pair of eyes and lips," Troyes sighed, "but sweetie, these new features now make your nose look too big. Maybe you can work on that."

The prince thanked Troyes and went inside for the book. He found the chapter about the nose and started drawing the thinnest, most symmetrical note on the last blank page of the chapter.

By the morning, the prince had a completely new face. He looked more like a caricature than a human being. The new facial features also created problems. The big blue eyes would burn constantly because the prince could hardly blink. His lips were so plump and stiff that he could not talk properly. And the new nose? Well, let's just say it should have come with a CPAP prescription.

The entourage of models and actors was at first good support, but after a while, each of them would offer critiques and suggest new changes – longer legs, lower hairlines, broader shoulders, etc. The prince could no longer tell if he looked any better. He was, in fact, miserable. The new body parts, though appeared more visually pleasing, were not functionally useful. The longer legs made him stumble and fall and his coordination was poor with the broader shoulders. He tried going out on dates again, but his new looks made him even more self-conscious and insecure, and all the dates went poorly.

One day, his model and actor friends were visiting. The prince lamented his lack of success in the dating scene. Fabio then said, "You need to be more muscular."

Kameron-Tiffany chimed in, "Yeah, and taller, you need to be taller."

Troyes, not to be left out, said to the prince, "And um, that nose. You are going to do something about that, right?"

The prince got very frustrated and said, "What more do you want me to do? All this is still not enough? I feel like I am a freak!" He broke down and cried. The prince's sadness and frustration made his beautiful friends uncomfortable, so they quickly excused themselves and left.

The prince thought of Jill. Besides himself, Jill was the only other person who knew about the book. Since she gave him the book, Jill had been watching the prince's changing appearances with great concern, and she felt very responsible. Jill rushed to the castle when she heard the prince was looking for her.

When she saw the prince, she tried her best to look unfazed. The prince had perfect eyes, nose, lips, cheekbones, and hairlines. But together, these perfections looked unnatural, and the prince looked totally unhappy. Jill had never seen such perfect features on such a sad face. She gave him a hug and held him tight in compassion. The prince then showed her the book. He explained to her how the book changed his appearance. Then he finally said, "I don't know what to do anymore. I really need your help."

Jill flipped past the pages of Part One. When she got to Part Two, which was titled "Formless", she asked the prince if he had gone through this part of the book.

The prince said no. All his focus had been on the chapters in Part One. Jill began going through the pages of Part Two. There was only one line written on the page.

"Remove pages from Part One to reveal the content in this chapter."

Jill looked at the prince, who had a determined look on his face. The prince found pages from the chapter about the eyes and tore them off the book.

Soon as the pages left the book, his eyes turned back into their natural shape and color. The prince could freely blink, and his eyes weren't watery all the time anymore.

When the prince turned the pages to Part Two, a new message appeared in the first chapter.

"Congratulations. If you read this message, it means you are ready to embark on the journey to formless beauty. To look beautiful, start from the inside."

The prince tore off more pages from the chapter about the mouth. His lips turned back to their natural form.

The prince could now smile and close his mouth completely. In Part Two, more lines appeared.

"Your beauty has everything to do with how you see yourself and much less to do with how you appear to others. The moment you decide to be yourself, you are beautiful."

More messages emerged as the prince removed chapters from Part One.

"Beauty is what the mind perceives. Troubled minds cling to attachments and are blinded to true beauty. True beauty is formless and lies in how we lead our lives with virtuous conduct, caring speech, and unadulterated mind."

The prince continued tearing off pages from Part One. By the time he finished, the prince turned back to how he used to look before he had the book in his possession – a regular-looking man. When he looked at the last page of Part Two, the final line read,

"You are enough."

He looked at Jill, who smiled back at him. The prince handed over what remained of the book to her.

"I am sorry I destroyed the library's book," said the prince with a guilty look.

"That's perfectly fine. Your well-being is more important. Welcome back, your highness," Jill said, then she asked, "are you going to be all right?"

The prince smiled, "I will be. I had so many faces and bodies the past few days, and I was not happy with a single one of them. Then I realized that my exterior was never the problem, it was my soul that needed a makeover. I needed to love myself and know that I am enough."

From then on, the prince stopped hanging out with models and actors. He started spending time with himself. When he felt like socializing, he would have tea with scholars and spiritual thinkers. He never saw Fabio, Kameron-Tiffany, or Troyes and his silent s again.

The End

> *There are two kinds of suffering. The first is what all beings go through when undesirable changes inevitably happen. The second kind of suffering is what we create in response to the first. Attachment is the fuel of the second kind of suffering. Attachment leads to unrealistic expectations, which lead to disappointments and more suffering. By allowing ourselves to let go of what is no longer our truth, we free ourselves from attachments and approach closer to freedom of mind.*

ABOUT THE AUTHOR

Petey Lao, MD is the person behind the name NahMo. This is Petey's first literary work. Before *Wake*, Petey had zero experience writing fiction or non-fiction. His full-time job is in the intensive care unit, where writing is not meant to be entertaining.

He is a practitioner of Theravada Buddhism. Petey lives in California with his husband and daughter. They have a very well-behaved Australian shepherd and three guinea pigs.

Lightning Source UK Ltd.
Milton Keynes UK
UKHW020730090223
416597UK00012B/635

9 798987 393000